THREE

W9-AYV-478

03

TURTLE ISLAND

JANE LOUISE CURRY

TURTLE ISLAND

TALES *of the* ALGONQUIAN NATIONS

Illustrated

by

JAMES WATTS

MARGARET K. MCELDERRY BOOKS

Margaret K. McElderry Books
An imprint of Simon & Schuster Children's Publishing Division
1230 Avenue of the Americas
New York, NY 10020

Book design by Michael Nelson
The text of this book is set in Guardi Roman.

Printed in the United States of America
10 9 8 7 6 5 4 3 2 1

Library of Congress Cataloging-in-Publication Data
Curry, Jane Louise.
Turtle Island: tales of the Algonquian nations / Jane Louise
Curry; illustrated by James Watts.—1st ed.
p. cm.
Includes bibliographical references.
Summary: A collection of twenty-seven tales from the different
tribes that are part of the Algonquian peoples who lived from the
Middle Atlantic states up through eastern Canada.
ISBN: 0-689-82233-2
1. Algonquian Indians—Folklore. 2. Tales—United States.
3. Tales—Canada. [1. Algonquian Indians—Folklore. 2. Indians
of North America—Folklore. 3. Folklore—North America.]
I. Watts, James, 1955–   ill. II. Title.
E99.A83C87   1999   398.2'089'973—dc21   98-20393

FIRST
EDITION

For Peter and Jerry and Joe
—J.L.C.

For Herbi, Martha, Maria, Theresa, and Anna Sophie
—J.W.

CONTENTS

ABOUT THE ALGONQUINS / ix

1. THE CREATOR MAKES THE WORLD *Lenapé* / 1

2. RAINBOW CROW *Lenapé* / 5

3. THE RACE BETWEEN BUFFALO AND MAN *Cheyenne* / 11

4. WHY DEER HAVE SHORT TAILS *Shawnee* / 18

5. THE THREE CRANBERRIES *Ojibway* / 21

6. THE COMING OF MANABUSH *Menomini* / 23

7. MANABUSH AND THE MONSTERS *Menomini* / 27

8. THE GREAT FLOOD *Ojibway* / 33

9. TURTLE ISLAND *Lenapé* / 36

10. MAUSHOP THE GIANT *Wampanoag/Pequot/Narraganset/ Montauk* / 40

11. WESAKAYCHAK SNARES THE SUN *Cree* / 44

12. BEAVER AND MUSKRAT CHANGE TAILS *Malecite* / 48

13. WESAKAYCHAK RIDES ON THE MOON *Cree* / 50

14. WOODPECKER AND SUGAR MAPLE *Lenapé* / 56

15. WHY BLACKFEET NEVER KILL MICE *Blackfoot* / 59

16. GROUND SQUIRREL AND TURTLE *Cheyenne* / 64

17. HOW SUMMER CAME TO THE NORTH *Naskapi* / 66

18. THE WHITE FAWN *Miami* / 71

19. THE GREAT BEAR HUNT *Fox* / 77

20. HOW GLOOSKAP DEFEATED THE GREAT BULLFROG
    Passamaquoddy / 81

21. THE LAND OF THE NORTHERN LIGHTS *Abenaki* / 89

22. THE SEVEN WISE MEN *Lenapé* / 93

23. THE BURNT-FACED GIRL *Micmac* / 98

24. THE BEAR MAIDEN *Ojibway* / 103

25. KUPAHWEESE'S LUCK *Lenapé* / 111

26. THE MIGHTY WASIS *Penobscot* / 116

27. GLOOSKAP'S FAREWELL GIFTS *Micmac/Passamaquoddy* / 120

ABOUT THE STORYTELLERS / 127

ABOUT THE STORIES / 139

ABOUT THE AUTHOR / 146

SoME of THE ALGONQUIAN PEOPLES

ABOUT THE ALGONQUINS

Traditions of the Algonquian peoples tell that in the far-off past, perhaps a thousand—or two, or three thousand—years ago, their ancestors came from a land of ice and snow far to the north and west. The Lenapé, whose name means "the real people" or "the original people," were held in great respect by the other Algonquins who traveled with them all those long years toward the east and called them "the Grandfathers" out of respect for their wisdom. Of the Algonquian tribes who did not cross the great river Mississippi with the Lenapé, some later remembered more of the old tales than the Grandfathers themselves did. Of those who traveled with the Lenapé to the great ocean in the east and afterward moved on to the south or north, some lost threads from the old tales, and some dressed theirs in new or borrowed feathers. That is the way of tales handed down through the years from storyteller to storyteller. Among the Algonquins, storytellers were great people. West or east, north or south, the tribes loved nothing better than a winter night, a campfire, and a story.

TURTLE ISLAND

THE CREATOR MAKES THE WORLD

Lenapé

Before the world was made, this earth was lost in fog and mist. It had no shape, no land, no seas. Only the Great Manito, the Great Spirit and Creator of all things, was here, and in the space above, and everywhere. Until he divided the land from the sky and made the sun and moon and stars, everything was darkness and confusion. Then the Creator gave the sun and the moon and each of the lights in the sky their places, and paths to follow. He raised up a great wind to blow away the mists and fogs, and to draw the waters together. The waters gathered to make the lakes and seas, and islands grew up in them. And the wind blew until the clear air sparkled.

Then the Great Manito gave a spirit to Sun and to Moon, and to the stars, and to Rock and Fire and Water, and Wind. The Wind he divided into four Winds, and made them Keepers of the Four Directions—North and South, East and West. Next, he made the great Thunder Beings, mighty 'manitos whose arrows can shatter trees. All of these spirits were manitos, but none was as great as the Creator.

Afterward, the Creator made the first men and women. They were very different from the men and

women of the Second World, which is the world we live in. They were as different from the Lenapé of today as the sun is from the moon, for those people of the Old Days had magic. Many had the strength and wisdom we see in animals, and later would learn to take on the shapes of animals.

Next, the Creator made the animals themselves. While he shaped the fish and turtles, the beasts and birds, the other manitos cared for the First Men and First Mothers. They showed them what to use for food when they were hungry, and taught them knowledge and how to play and be glad. And the animals and men lived as friends, for they were alike in many ways.

But not all creatures lived as friends.

Somehow, in secret, the evil manito Matantu found the earth. He made himself a country in the world below the earth, in the waters and the hollows under the earth. He, too, was a maker, and powerful, and he took on the shape of a great horned snake. He made the flies, and gnats, and monsters. He brought badness, and quarrels, and misery. He brought tornadoes and earthquakes, and sickness and death. He hated the thought of wisdom and good friends and gladness, and so he plotted and made war against all men and women and children, to try to take these good things away from them.

The wicked Matantu gathered with him, in the World Below, the snakes and monsters, and all of the animals he could teach to hate Man. Even now, they listen in secret to men and their words, and wish to punish those who tell tales about them. Because the Lenapé and their Grandchildren know this, they tell stories only in the wintertime, around a campfire. In winter, wicked creatures—and mischief makers like the Little People of the forest—seek out the darkness and sleep, and it is safe to tell stories.

Rainbow Crow

Lenapé

In the Old Days of the First Men and First Mothers, when the animal people first moved out across the new-made world, the earth and its waters were warm. The sun shone. Green things grew and flowered in the fields and forests. The animals ate well, and all, even Rabbit and Panther, lived together as friends.

One day, to the animals' surprise, the sky turned gray and the air cold. Soft white flakes drifted down from the sky. At first, the flakes vanished as they touched the trees or grass or Fox's fur. Soon they came faster and more thickly. They covered the ground like a blanket of goose down.

The strange white flakes tasted like cold water. The animals were curious, but did not fear them. Not at first. But when the animals looked for Mouse and could not find him until they spied the tip of his tail, they began to be alarmed.

Soon the cry went up, "Who has seen Rabbit?" They looked for him everywhere, and only found him when they spied his ears sticking up from the snow. Then they were frightened.

"When will it stop?" they asked, and they called

all of the animals to a council to decide what they should do.

"Hoo!" said Owl. "We cannot stop the Whiteness-falling-from-the-sky. Only Kishelamákank, the Creator, can stop it. Someone must carry our fears up to the Creator, and ask that He stop its falling."

"But who will go?" the animals asked. "It is a long way up the sky to the lodge of the Creator, and a hard climb."

Opossum spoke up first. "Owl is the wisest of us. Surely he should go."

The animals whispered among themselves. "Owl *is* wisest," they said at last, "but he sees best in the dark. Our messenger must travel both by night and by day. Owl might lose his way in the brightness of day."

"That is so," Beaver said. "I say Raccoon should go. He can see well by night or by day."

"No, not Raccoon!" exclaimed the others. They thought Raccoon too silly. "He might trot off after his tail instead of his nose," they said.

"Yes," agreed Skunk. "Let us choose a better sniffer, someone with a good, sharp nose. Let us have Coyote!"

"No, no, no!" cried everyone else. "Who has ever seen Coyote follow a trail for as long as half a day? He is forever turning aside to play pranks. He might try to gobble up the wind, or go chasing clouds up and down the sky."

No! Yes! No! The animals' argument grew louder and louder. They squawked and yapped and howled. They squeaked and hissed and growled, and still could not decide who should carry their message to the Great Spirit. All the while, the snow grew deeper and deeper. The mice and squirrels, the lizards and rabbits, had to climb on top of the deer and bears and wolves and moose, but still they all argued. "Can we never agree?" Owl groaned.

Just as they were about to give up finding a messenger, a call rang down from the tallest tree. "I will go!"

The voice they heard was as sweet as honey, as bright as the sunshine, and as clear as fresh water. The animals looked up in wonder, and saw that it was Rainbow Crow who called. The beautiful colors of his feathers shimmered as he floated down to join them.

"I will go," he said again.

The animals were happy to have so fine a messenger. They gave Rainbow Crow a great cheer, and sang their thanks as he rose into the sky.

Rainbow Crow flew high. He soared up through the snow and left the clouds below at sunset. He floated up the path past the moon. On the second day, he sailed past the stars. At the end of the third day, he came to the land and the lodge of the Creator. Alas, the Great Spirit was too busy keeping watch over the worlds below to see him.

So Rainbow Crow drew a deep breath and began to sing. He sang of the sun and moon and stars, and the beauty of his own world. The Creator of the sun and moon and stars and the World Below looked up and listened.

"Rainbow Crow," He said when the song was sung, "I thank you for so beautiful a gift. In all of my Creation I have not heard a sweeter voice or sweeter song. No gift I can give you in thanks would match it. Is there anything you wish?"

"Great Manito," said Rainbow Crow, "there is. The snow has been snowing for days in our world below the clouds. It will not stop. Soon it will be so deep that even the tallest moose will disappear. I came to ask you to stop its falling."

"Ah, Rainbow Crow, I cannot. As the wind has its own spirit, so does the snow. The snow will stop when the Snow Spirit decides to follow the Wind Spirit to the east, but even then the world will be cold."

"But you can stop the cold," said Rainbow Crow. "I choose that for my gift."

"Alas, I cannot. But I can give you something to warm you until the days are sunnier." The Creator took a stick and reached down to touch it to the sun. When flames lit its tip, He held it out to Rainbow Crow. "It is called fire," He said, as Rainbow Crow took it in his beak. "It can melt snow, too. But you must hurry back to the earth before the flames die. It is a gift I will give only once. So, fly!"

At once Rainbow Crow, with a strong flap of his wings, lifted up, and then soared downward toward the earth.

On that first day, the stick burned steadily, but sparks and smoke flew back to burn and stain Rainbow Crow's tail feathers.

On the second day, as the stick grew shorter, the flames grew longer. The dark soot covered all his feathers.

On the third day, the flames burned the stick down to a stub. All the while, the hot smoke so choked poor Rainbow Crow that he could scarcely breathe. At last, he reached the earth and the clearing where he had left the animals. The snow had stopped, but there were only a few treetops showing. Rainbow Crow perched on the tallest of these, and clutched the burning stub of stick in one claw.

"Caw! Caw!" he cried out.

His voice was so hoarse that at first he did not know it was his own. "Caw! Caw!" he cried again, but no answer came. The animals were buried from sight, every one.

So Rainbow Crow took up the firestick again in his beak, and flew low over the snow that covered the clearing. Around and around he flew. The snow began to melt. Soon he saw Moose's great antlers, then Bear's broad back and, at last, Mouse's ears. Moose's antlers gave a shake, Bear's back a shiver, and Mouse's ears a twitch, and Rainbow Crow knew that all was well.

The shivering animals gathered a great heap of firewood, and Rainbow Crow lit it with the last spark of the Great Spirit's gift. But while the animals danced around the fire and praised him, Rainbow Crow flew back to the treetops and wept. His beautiful voice was gone. His beautiful rainbow colors were gone. He was only a hoarse black crow.

High above, the Creator heard his weeping and came down from the sky to comfort him. "Soon," the Great Spirit said, "there will be men in the world. They will be masters of fire and animals. You alone will be free. Man will not hunt you for your meat, for it has the taste of smoke. He will not capture you to sing to him, or so that he can steal your fine feathers, for he will not hear what I hear, or see what I see. I hear the sound of your courage, and I see all the colors of the rainbow in your shiny black feathers."

Crow spread out one wing and looked. Suddenly he, too, saw the rainbow shimmer, and that it was beautiful, and he was pleased. The Creator smiled and returned to the sky. Crow went back to his friends, to enjoy their thanks and to preen his handsome feathers.

The Race between Buffalo and Man

Cheyenne

Long ago, in the Old Time, after Maheo, the Great Spirit, first made the earth and made animals and men to live on it, the animals were people, too. All of the peoples were equal, and everyone enjoyed this new, green world.

It was not long, though, before the buffalo began to grumble.

"We buffalo are the biggest animals on earth, and the strongest," said Buffalo Chief. "Who are these others, with their fur and feathers and foolish bare skin, that they should be our equals? Or men, that they should be chief over us? They should bow their heads before us. They should honor us as greatest of all."

"Hoh! Yes!" cried the buffalo young men. "All creatures with eyes to see, must see it! Yet they strut up and down the land as if they were as tall as we, and had shoulders as strong. How can men and women with their puny necks, and their two little legs, and their hairless skins, act as if they were as great as we."

Buffalo Chief agreed. "Hoh! The weakest buffalo girl is stronger than any man who walks the earth. Come, let us pay these people a visit. Let us tell them that from this day on, they are to be our servants." And so the buffalo thundered off toward the village of men.

In the village, it was the time of the Sun Dance. Men and women and children were camped in a wide circle around the Sun Dance lodge. The buffalo trotted into the center of the circle, and when the dust their hooves raised had settled, Buffalo Chief stepped up to the lodge.

The Sun Dance shaman sat inside the eastern door. "Enter, Friend Buffalo," he said. "Enter and be welcome."

Buffalo Chief scowled. "Why do you wish us to come in?" he boomed.

The shaman was surprised. "Because we are friends. All of our friends may watch the dance, and join in it if they wish."

Buffalo Chief tossed his great head. "We have no wish to join in. We are not your friends. We are your masters. We are the strongest people on earth, and we have come to tell you so."

The shaman shook his head. "That cannot be. The Great Spirit taught us that all creatures are friends and brothers."

Buffalo Chief snorted. "Nonsense! How can you look at us, and not see that we are greater than all others? Shall we prove it to you with a race? Choose your fastest runner, and the weakest of our women will pass him as if he stood still."

The Sun Dance shaman shook his head. "Our young men are weak. To make themselves pure for the dance, they have gone without food and water for four days. If we must race, let it be a relay race, four runners to a side. The other animals and the birds can choose which of them will run, and whether they will run for buffalo or man."

Buffalo Chief turned to the buffalo young men. "What do you say of this plan?"

The buffalo shrugged their great shoulders and nodded their great heads all together. "It is fair," they said.

"Then it is agreed. Five days from today we shall race," said Buffalo Chief. "Send word to all of the birds and all of the animals. Let them choose sides."

So runners were sent in every direction, east and west and north and south. All of the animals except the fish agreed to come. "How can we?" asked the fish. "It is not a swimming race. We cannot race on dry land." But the others came. On the fourth day, they came to the Sun Dance camp and set up their tipis in a great circle around the circle of men and women. On the fifth day everyone gathered at the Sun Dance lodge to choose the relay teams.

The buffalo were surprised and pleased when Elk and Deer and Antelope chose to run on their team. "O-hoh!" rumbled Buffalo Chief. "All of the split-hoofed people, the fast runners, are with us!"

"Who will run for the human people, the men and women?" the shaman cried out to the crowd.

Dog stepped forward. "I will. You are my friends. You feed and care for me, and I love to run with you."

"Who else is with us?" asked the shaman.

The youngest of the Sun Dancers joined Dog. "I am not tired from the dancing. I will run for my people."

"I, too," said Eagle. "Men wear my feathers to honor me. I shall race to honor men."

"And so shall I," said Hawk.

When the rules were agreed, the shaman and Buffalo Chief settled on a course for the race. Posts were set up along its curve, to mark the places where each pair of runners would wait. Elk and the Sun Dancer stood ready at the starting line. Dog and Deer took their places at the second post. Antelope and Eagle were third. Hawk and Buffalo Woman went to wait at the last relay post.

When Buffalo Woman went by on her way to her post, the men and women and dogs and birds had to hide their laughter. She had wide shoulders and a broad chest. Her wild, frizzy hair made her big head look even bigger, but her waist and rear were small. Her legs were almost as skinny as twigs. The people wondered why she did not fall forward onto her nose. Only when they saw Hawk walking with her, did they begin to worry. His wings were folded at his sides, and he looked tiny and weak beside her.

When all was ready, Buffalo Chief and the shaman beat on the drum. Elk and the young Sun Dancer dashed off. The young man ran his best, but Elk soon was far ahead. When Dog's turn came, Deer was already so far away that Dog could not catch up, even though his paws flew so fast that they barely touched the ground. In the third relay, Antelope was the faster, but Eagle the stronger. Antelope began to tire first, and he and Eagle were even as they came to the fourth post. Hawk and Buffalo Woman set off neck and neck.

Buffalo Woman dashed away first. She was young, and her spindly legs flashed faster and faster. She was proud to be running for the honor of the Greatest People of All. But then Hawk spread his great wings and rose into the air. He soared along on the wind, and kept even with Buffalo Woman with only a flap or two of his wings. Ahead of them, a great crowd waited at the finish line at the foot of the mountains. Buffalo Woman ran faster still. Only then did Hawk truly begin to beat his wings. When Buffalo Woman crossed the line, Hawk was already past it, and sitting on the tallest mountain peak.

The men and their friends cheered. Buffalo Chief groaned. Never again could he say, "We are the greatest of all creatures on earth!" The buffalo and split-hoofed people turned and trotted away, downhearted, their eyes on the ground. They could not even say that they were greater than the birds of the air.

To the elk and the deer and the antelope people, Buffalo Chief said, "Take care! Now Man will hunt us all for food. He will use our hides for clothing and blankets, and for coverings for his tipis." And so each of the split-hoofed people went their own way, and they feared Man.

Back at the finish line, Hawk floated down to join the men and dogs and their bird and animal friends. The people shouted "Ho-*yoh!*" and "Hawk! Hawk!" for because of him, men were still their own masters. The First Men honored Hawk as greater even than Eagle.

And in the World that was still to come, the Cheyenne people remembered all this and, to honor him, named the greatest of their soldiers the Hawk Soldiers.

WHY DEER HAVE SHORT TAILS

Shawnee

Long ago, in the days of the First People, a sister came to live with her brother in his wigwam in a clearing in the forest, far from the lodges of other people. All went well until the day her brother said, "This morning I must go hunting, for we have no meat."

Before he went, he dipped a small bowl into the leather water bucket to fill it, and then placed it on the floor by the wall.

"Hear me, my sister," he said. "Do not drink the water in the dish, but look at it from time to time. If I am killed by beasts or enemies while I am hunting, the water will turn red to warn you. And hear this, too: When you parch the corn, whatever you do, do not parch the little blue ears in the large red basket." He did not explain, but took up his bow and arrows and went off into the forest.

When he was gone, the sister looked at the baskets of corn and began to wonder. Why must she not parch the little blue ears? She took down the red basket from the place where it hung and peered inside. "What is your secret, little ears?" she said. "You are only corn. Why should I not parch you?"

She put the basket back, but she could think of

nothing else, and soon took it down again. She poured out the little ears and shelled the little kernels off their cobs. Then she took a handful to the fire.

Over the fire, the corn began to pop. The kernels hopped, and popped, and puffed up, large and white. They smelled so good that her mouth watered. They tasted so good that she popped more. She popped and ate, and popped and popped, and the lodge began to fill with white corn. She could not eat fast enough, and she could not reach the fire to rake the kernels from the cooking stone. Soon the popcorn crowded her flat against the wall.

Then she heard the deer coming.

They smelled the corn.

The deer crowded up to the door and began to eat, and their long tails switched happily behind them. More and more came, and as the deer in front ate their way into the lodge, others came crowding behind. They ate and ate and ate until every last crumb of popcorn was gone. Then they looked for something more to eat. The sister was hidden under a fur blanket, and when she trembled they saw the blanket shiver.

"Come out and stand before me!" the chief of the deer commanded, and she did. When the chief saw that she was young and beautiful, he wished to have her for his own. "You will come with us, and be my wife," he said, and the other deer lifted her up with their antlers to perch her on the chief's. Then the great deer dashed off into the forest with the hunter's sister riding on his antlers, and the deer people ran after them.

When the brother returned, he saw that the red basket was empty, and his sister gone. "O-hoh!" he cried, and he called aloud for help from the spirits. Two big black spirit-snakes came at his call, and he said, "Wise Ones, take me to find my sister!"

"We will," they said. So they took him up, a foot on each of their backs, and flew off with him into the forest. They followed the deer all day and all night. In the morning, they came to the clearing where the deer lived. The bucks were as frightened as the does, for the deer people were not warriors. They bowed their heads and stuck their antlers in the ground, and cried out, "Oh, do not kill us! Do not kill us!"

"Very well, I will not," the angry brother said as his sister leaped down from her antler chair. Instead, he kicked each deer so hard on the rear that its tail flew off, and that is why the tails of deer are short today.

But that was not all, for the hunter's sister had not obeyed his warning about the blue corn. Sadly, he led her home, and there he painted her legs red. At once she was turned into a duck, and with a sad *"Quack-uack!"* she waddled off to paddle in the creek. Her brother put on the shape of a wolf and afterward spent all his days in hunting. Those two never were people again.

THE THREE CRANBERRIES

Ojibway

One winter long ago, three cranberry sisters and their new husbands lived in a lodge in the woods. One pretty cranberry was green, one white, and one red. At first the three sisters thought it pleasant to be warm indoors with their husbands while the snow fell, but soon the ground was covered. Before long, they had eaten up all their food. The next morning, the husbands took up their bows and arrows, tied on their snowshoes, and went out to hunt.

The three cranberries had never before been left alone. Their fire was warm, but they began to shiver with fear. "Oh, Sister!" they cried to one another. "What shall we do if a wolf comes?"

"I will climb up the spruce tree that stands by the lodge door," squeaked the green one.

"I," piped up the white one, "will jump into the kettle of boiled hominy. In there, no one will see that I am a cranberry."

"And I," said the red one, "will hide my bright color under the snow."

By and by, wolves did come through the woods. When the three cranberries heard them, they ran and hid as they had planned.

Only one of the three had planned wisely. The wolves rushed at the door and trampled the red one under the snow beside the path, so that it was spotted red with her juice. In the lodge, they dashed straight to the kettle that sat by the fire. They gobbled up the hominy, white cranberry and all. But the wolves never saw the green one, for she clung to a high branch in the green spruce tree, and only she was saved.

To be wise is to keep well out of the wolf's way.

THE COMING OF MANABUSH

Menomini

In those Old Days, when men as well as manitos could take the shape of animals, and animals were much like men, there lived an old woman on an island in the middle of a lake. Her name was Nokomis, which means "Grandmother," and she had an unlucky daughter so beautiful that the West Wind fell in love with her. After a time, the daughter of Nokomis had twin baby sons. One was a boy and the other a wolf pup, and no sooner were they born than the daughter died, both she and the little wolf pup.

Grandmother's heart ached. She wept many tears for her beautiful daughter. She wrapped the tiny boy in soft, dry grass, and covered him with a wooden bowl to protect him. Then she carried her daughter and the little wolf to their burying place. When she returned, she sat down again to weep and to wail. For four days she wept, until on the fourth day she heard a little knocking noise. She followed the noise to the corner of her wigwam, and there was the wooden bowl. The bowl moved and knocked against the lodge pole.

"Grandson!" Nokomis cried. "I have forgotten you!" And she lifted up the bowl.

Under it sat a tiny white rabbit, its ears and nose aquiver.

Nokomis picked the rabbit up, and cupped it in the palm of her hand. "Oh, dear little rabbit," she sang. "My Great Rabbit, my Manabush." And so he was named, but he has many names, for each of the languages of the Grandchildren of the Lenapé is different in some way. The Lenapé call him Nanabush or Nanapush, and he is to other peoples Manabozho, Nanaboso, Nenebojo, Wisaka, Wesakaychak, Glooskap, Old-Man, the Trickster, and many other names.

As Nokomis sang, the love she felt for Manabush dried her tears, and she fed him and cared for him. On the day that little Manabush sat up and for the first time hopped across the floor, the earth shook under his feet. "Hoh, little Manabush!" his grandmother cried. "The earth knows that you will grow up to do great deeds!"

Not only the earth knew. In the places beneath the earth, the evil spirits and monsters felt the earth tremble.

"What was that?" they cried.

"Somewhere in the earth above, a great manito is born," said some.

"Then we must find where he lives and destroy him," cried the others.

But Manabush was wiser than they, even when he was young, and he grew to be a man. When he was

grown, he took more often the shape of a man than a rabbit, for he had learned why the Great Spirit sent him to earth. He was to teach the men and women many things that they needed to know to live well. He showed them good plants for food, and medicines to cure disease and keep death from coming too soon. These and many other good things he taught them.

At last, when his work was done, Manabush decided to leave the villages of men and to find a place where he could live by himself. For many days he traveled through the forest, and at last came to a great lake. There, he built a lodge at the edge of the water, and then settled down to watch the days pass by.

The manitos of the earth and air saw this, and shook their heads. "It is not good that Manabush should live alone and forget how to care for others," some said.

"It is not wise that Manabush should live alone beside the wide water, for monsters dwell there," said others.

"Shall we give back to the Great Rabbit his wolf brother?" they asked.

It was soon agreed, and done. The manitos brought Manabush's twin brother, Moque'o the Wolf, to life in his human shape. They led him to the lodge by the lake, where Manabush welcomed him with great joy. From that day, the brothers lived happily together, and Moque'o became a great hunter.

MANABUSH AND THE MONSTERS

Menomini

Manabush knew that the evil manitos and the monsters who lived under the lake beside his house hated him. He knew that they wished to destroy him. He was careful to keep out of their reach, and he warned Moque'o the Wolf of their anger.

"Take care, my brother," he said, "for to hurt me, they would happily hurt you. The lake is beautiful, but take care. If you hunt on the other side of the lake, never swim home to save time. No matter how late, go the long way around, by the shore. Do not even put a paw in the water." He said this because Moque'o always hunted in his wolf shape.

"I will be careful," Moque'o promised. "I do my hunting in the forest, far from the lake. I will be safe."

Moque'o took care, but one day in winter, when the snow was deep, the deer he followed led him toward the lake. After the Wolf ate, the hour was late, and he saw that the lake was frozen over.

"Hoh!" he thought. "It is too far to go the long way around by the shore. I can cross the ice and never put a paw in the water."

And so he did. But he was only halfway to the lodge on the far side when the ice creaked, and cracked, and broke. As soon as his paws touched the water, the bad manitos and monsters snatched at him and pulled him under.

In that same moment, Manabush knew what had happened. His heart was sore, and for four days he groaned in his grief. Each time he groaned or sighed, the earth shook and new hills raised up all around. On the fifth day, the shadow of Moque'o the Wolf came to Manabush, and Manabush knew that this time his brother could not come back to life.

"Brother," he said, "my heart hurts to lose you, but now you must walk the path of the sun into the sky in the west. When you reach the hunting ground in the heavens, you will be chief of all the shadows in that place. Someday, I will come and be with you there." So he bid the shadow farewell, and Moque'o went.

Afterward, Manabush went far away. He hid himself, putting on his little white rabbit shape when he did not wish men to see him. While he was hidden, he dreamed of a plan to punish the wicked manitos of the lake and the underground world for killing his brother. To make the plan work, he called upon the Thunderers for help. The Thunder Brothers heard his prayer, and flew down from the Land in the Sky to ask why he had called them.

"I have made a plan," Manabush told them. "If I am to make the Great Horned Snake and his manitos and monsters pay for killing my brother, I must trick them into leaving the water. I must bring them up onto the land, into the air."

"*How* will you trick them?" the Thunder Brothers asked.

"You shall trick them for me, if you will," Manabush said. "Tell the waterbirds, and all the animals who fish in the lake, that you wish to challenge the manitos below to a new game. The game, you will tell them, is played with a ball and sticks. Say you will meet them where the sandy shore beside the lake is widest."

"And when they come?" asked the Thunderers.

"When they come, you will play the game I teach you. I will do the rest," Manabush answered. "Afterward the game will be yours, if you like, to play all day in the sky."

So the Thunderers agreed. They told the waterbirds and the animals who fished in the lake about the time and place for the ball game. They laughed and said, "We will beat the manitos of the Land Below as easily as if they were children!" When the waterbirds and the fishers told all this to the manitos under the water, the bad manitos and monsters made the water bubble and froth with their anger.

"Of course we will go," they growled to each other. "And after we win, we will destroy the proud Thunder Boys!"

On the day of the game, Manabush climbed a tall tree in the forest nearby to watch. While the players played, the two chiefs from the Land Below—two great white water bears—stretched themselves out in the sunshine on the bank beside the playing field. "Hoh-oh!" Manabush thought to himself, and he marked the place in his mind.

The game went on from morning until evening. Neither team scored a goal, so they agreed to return the next day. The next morning, as the players chose their sticks for the game, the two bear manitos from the Land Below returned to the bank where they had lain the day before.

"Hoh! Was that tree here yesterday?" one asked the other.

The second bear chief looked at the pine tree that stood a few feet away. Its top was cut off halfway up, and its two strongest branches drooped over their heads.

"No, it was not," he said.

"Arghh!" the first bear chief growled. "Then it is a trick. It is our enemy, Manabush."

"The pine tree?" asked a Thunderer passing by. "How can it be? It has been there for years." They began to argue, the bad manitos saying, "No," and the Thunder Brothers, "Yes."

"Enough!" roared the two white water bears. "We shall see," they said. So they called for Grizzly

Bear. Grizzly Bear came, and he climbed the tree and began to rip the bark off with his claws. Manabush—for the tree was Manabush—held his breath and bore the pain. He did not even twitch.

The bad manitos still did not trust the tree. They called out over the water to the Great Horned Serpent.

The lake shivered at their call. The Great Horned Serpent, which could be as small as a worm or bigger than the largest snake in the world, raised up his huge horned head and sliced through the water like an arrow through air. He slithered up onto the shore, and both the Thunderers and the bad manitos drew back as he passed. When he came to the tree, he wrapped his coils around the trunk from the foot to the top, and drew them tight. He squeezed and squeezed. Manabush, strong as he was, was almost strangled, but he did not cry out. At last the Great Horned Serpent gave up and slithered back to the lake.

The bear chiefs grumbled. "If the tree is not Manabush, it is not," they said at last. So they sat down under its branches and watched as the ball game began again.

At once the Thunderers carried the ball on their ball sticks to the far end of the field. The wicked manitos raised their sticks and rushed after them, and the great bear manitos were left alone under the tree. Swiftly the Manabush-Tree set an arrow to his bow and, with his twig fingers, drew it taut and shot the first chief. His second arrow shot the second evil manito.

"For my brother, Wolf!" Manabush shouted in a great voice as he changed back into his human shape and headed for home.

THE GREAT FLOOD

Ojibway

On his way home from the ball game, Nanabozho—
for that is what the Ojibway call Manabush—sang of
the trick he had played to revenge his brother's death.
He had not gone far along the lakeshore when he
heard someone else singing. A little farther on, he
spied a large gray toad come walking out of the
woods. The ugly toad swung a club in one hand, carried a sack over his shoulder with the other, and
boomed out his song at the top of his voice.

"Hoh, Friend Toad!" called Nanabozho. "Where
do you go in such a noisy hurry, and what do you
carry in your sack?"

The toad gave him an unfriendly look. "I carry
medicines I have gathered," he croaked. "That rascal
Nanabozho has wounded our manito chiefs. I go to
the land under the lake to cure them. Who are you
who asks?"

"Who am I, Rascal Toad? I am that rascal, Nanabozho," he said, and with one blow he struck the
toad dead. Then Nanabozho changed himself into a
large gray toad. He picked up the sack and the club
and walked into the lake, singing a toad song at the
top of his voice.

When Nanabozho came to the bottom of the lake,

he walked along, singing his toad song, until he came to a place where the water manitos and monsters were playing at games. When they heard the singing and saw the toad, they stopped and called out, "What do you want, Toad? Why are you here?"

"I was sent for to doctor your chiefs," answered Nanabozho-Toad. "My medicines will stop their moaning and quiet their pains."

"That is good," the monsters said, and they showed him the doorway to the cavern where the chiefs were.

"Now, leave us," croaked Nanabozho-Toad. "I must be alone with the Great Ones, or my medicines and magic will not work."

So the water manitos and monsters went back to their games. When they were gone, Nanabozho went to look at the wounded enemies of the Creator and of all good creatures. Because of the tough hides of the chiefs of the Land Below, his arrows had done only half their work. Quickly, Nanabozho gave a hard push on each arrow and finished them off. Then he slipped out the door and sped up to the shore.

Under the lake behind him, the water manitos and beasts discovered how they had been fooled. The waters began to roil and boil. The monsters rose up from the waters and raced after Nanabozho, but he was already far away, and faster than they.

"Waters, run!" they roared. "Lake, rise up and swallow Nanabozho the Trickster, for he has killed our chiefs. Follow after him! Punish him! Pull him under!"

And the waters rose. And rose. They poured across the dry land and through the forest. They rolled over the hills to fill the valleys, and spilled out across the lands beyond. Nanabozho ran like the Four Winds, but the waters drew closer. He fled from the hills to the foothills of the mountains, and the waters still came. He ran from the foothills into the mountains, and they licked at his heels. All of the waters of the earth ran after him. Nanabozho reached the top of the highest mountain, and still they rose. He ran to the tallest of the pine trees on the mountaintop and began to climb it, but at each step he took upward, the waters swallowed the branch below. At last, he came to the treetop. And there all the waters of the earth and under the earth could not follow him.

There were not waters enough. They had covered the earth, and could rise no higher.

Nanabozho looked around him and saw that all the First World was buried under the waters. Animals struggled in the water nearby. Nanabozho called to them, and those who could, swam to the tree and joined him in the treetop.

Then Nanabozho looked out across the waters and sighed.

"The world is gone," he said. "I must make a new world, and new men to live in it with us."

Turtle Island

Lenapé

Nanabush, and all of the creatures who had not drowned, clung to the branches at the top of the tree. There were not many of them, but they weighted it down. "Our world is drowned! We are doomed!" they wailed. "Not even Nanabush can make a new world out of nothing."

Nanabush did not hear them, for as he watched and listened, he spied a low, dark shape far off on the waters. It was a shape that made his heart glad.

"See who comes!" he cried. They all looked, and saw that it was a turtle. From afar off, the turtle looked small, but the nearer it swam, the larger it grew. It swam straight for Nanabush's treetop, as straight as if it had been called.

The turtle was ancient, as old as it was large, and the animals saw that its shell was as mossy as the bank of a stream. "Come!" Nanabush called as it edged closer still. "Jump!" he cried, and he jumped to the turtle's back. The animals leaped after him. Together, they slithered and slipped on the wet green moss as they climbed to the top. When they reached it, the turtle turned and swam on.

"I shall make us a new world," said Nanabush,

"but we must have earth to make more earth. Since all of it is at the bottom of the waters, we need a good diver."

"Ask Loon," the animals said. "We can only dive from the Great Turtle's back, but Loon can dive from the air."

"Good," said Nanabush, and when the turtle had come to a stop in the sea, Nanabush asked Loon to dive deep. "We need only a little bit of earth," he said. "You can bring back enough in your beak."

So the brave bird dove, and the animals watched and waited. After a long while, Loon reappeared with a gasp and a sputter, and a flutter of wet wings.

"There is no bottom," Loon wheezed in a breathless whisper. "Or, if there is, it is too deep for me."

"There must be earth somewhere," the animals cried loudly, for they were afraid.

"There must be," agreed Nanabush. "When Loon is rested, he can fly out over the waters to look for it."

And Loon did. He flew for days, and rested on the waters at night, and was gone so long that the animals on the Great Turtle's back began to lose hope. When at last he came back, his feathers were rough and ragged, and his eyes rimmed with red, and he shivered with weariness.

But in his beak he carried a bit of good brown earth.

Nanabush smoothed his feathers, and soothed his shivers. "Brave Loon," he said, "you have saved us."

When he was rested, Loon guided the giant turtle toward the last bit of land, which was so high that the water barely washed over it. The Great Turtle, when he reached it, swam close, then climbed up and settled himself firmly upon it. He was so large that he covered it completely, and the edge of his shell touched the water. Then Nanabush took the earth that Loon had brought, and spread it over the turtle's shell, and it grew and spread out all around. That is why the Lenapé call this earth they live on Turtle Island.

And when the earth quakes, they say, it is the Great Turtle, moving in his sleep.

Maushop the Giant

Wampanoag/Pequot/Narraganset/Montauk

After the Great Flood, the giant Maushop, whom some called Wetucks, walked along the southern shore of the east-land. He found it bare, and still flat and soft underfoot.

"Hoh!" said Maushop to himself. "With a bit of work, this could be a good place."

At once, he began to form and plant it. He treaded it down with his feet, shaped it up with his hands, and sowed seeds. When he had finished his work, the land bore the shape it has still, with hills and valleys, rivers and bays, trees and all things green and growing.

When the work was finished, Maushop had land left over from dredging out the rivers and bays. He had nowhere else to put it, so he threw it into the sea, where it made a large island. There, in the island cliffs, he hollowed out a home for himself and his giant-wife, whose name was Squant.

Maushop and Squant ate well. If they felt like feasting on bear, Maushop waded across to the mainland to hunt. When the bears saw him coming, they ran for the tallest trees they could see and climbed them. Maushop wasn't bothered a bit. He reached up and knocked them off with his fist.

Once in a while one climbed so high that he had to use a club, but he always bagged his bear.

When Maushop and Squant were truly hungry, they ate seafood. Maushop swam out to sea in the morning, and at midday came swimming back, pulling a string of large fishes or a whale behind him. Between the two of them, they ate so much that their giant cookfire burned half the day. In the winter, it burned all day and night to warm them in their den. To feed the flames, Maushop pulled up trees for firewood. After dinner, he and his wife sat by the fire and smoked their pipes. When Maushop was done, he tapped out the ashes from his pipe over the water, always in the same spot. After a time that heap of ashes grew into the island that the people called Nantucket.

Men came to the east-land not long after Maushop and Squant. They built villages along the sea and inland, and called themselves the Eastern People. Some came to the island. These people, and all those who came after, were frightened when they saw Maushop emerge from his den at sunrise, for he stretched himself with a great rumble and groan before he swam out to sea.

"We must please this giant," they said to each other, "or he might eat us instead of the bears or whales."

From that time on, each time Maushop passed by a village, the bravest men came out and carried to him a gift of meat, of deer or raccoon or turkey. Each time, Maushop bent down and took the gifts carefully between his thumb and first finger, and walked on. The people knew that they had pleased him, for the next time he went whaling, he returned with two whales, and left one on the shore for them.

In this fashion, they lived together in peace for many years, with fear and peace offerings on the one side, and now and again a whale on the other. Maushop and Squant had two sons, and the villages of men grew in number. All was well until the middle of one hard, hard winter, when not a tree was to be found on the island for firewood. Every tree had been consumed in the giants' campfire. The Wampanoags on the island say that after the giants' fire burned out, poor Maushop froze to death. They say that his sons saved themselves by turning into killer whales, and Squant burrowed deep under the sand dunes, where on some days men still see the smoke from her cookfire and pipe. Others say that Maushop lived on, that he turned Squant into the great rock that men call Sakonnet, off the mainland coast, and then, like his sons, swam away.

One day many long ages afterward, the Pequot people on the mainland saw a huge, strange shape pass along their coast, and they took it for the giant

Maushop-Wetucks, swimming home at last. They raised a shout of "Hoh, Wetucks! Wetucks has come back to us!"

They soon knew that they were wrong. What they saw was a giant canoe with many strange white wings, floating on the water. The canoe carried men, many men in strange clothing, with strange white faces.

In the years to come, there were many more such great canoes.

And Maushop the Giant never did return.

WESAKAYCHAK SNARES THE SUN

Cree

After the Flood, when Wesakaychak—as the Cree called Manabush—had remade the land, the animals moved out across the earth. There they found that nothing worked as well as it had in the First World. Worst of all was the Sun. On some days, it came up at noon. On many, it never came up at all. When it did rise, it climbed so high that it gave no heat. Snow fell, and did not melt. Plants struggled to grow, and could not. Food was hard to find for everyone from Bee to Bear. Wesakaychak still had work to do.

He thought long and hard. "I have it!" he said at last. "I must catch the Sun. Then I must tie it down to the earth." So he took a long, strong cord and made a large snare. This snare he spread in the Sun's path. The next time the Sun rose, it was caught fast before it could climb too high. The more it struggled, the tighter the cord held. The Sun could not even burn it loose.

The animals shouted when they saw the Sun shine so brightly. They cheered when they saw the snow melt. But before long their cheers turned to groans. The Sun could not set. It hung above the trees day after day. Everything green began to shrivel. The animals began to wilt.

"The Sun is too hot!"

"It is too close!"

"It never goes down!"

"It will roast us all!"

"Cut it loose," they all cried together. The bravest took knives and tried, but the heat was too fierce. None could get close enough to cut the cord.

"Wesakaychak, this is your doing," the animals accused. "You must undo it."

Wesakaychak called Anaynake, the spirit of the Sun. "Great Anaynake," he cried. "If I set you free, will you promise to rise every morning and to set every evening? Will you ride all day in the middle sky, neither too low or too high, to warm the earth?"

"How can I promise?" Anaynake asked. "How can I warm the earth if Keewatin, the North Wind, blows? Where he blows, icicles and snowdrifts grow."

"That is true," Wesakaychak agreed. "North Wind must join our council."

Keewatin, the North Wind, came at Wesakaychak's call. The three manitos talked together, and an answer was agreed among them. North Wind and the Sun would each have a share of the year, and in the seasons in between, one would day by day give way to the other. "It shall be so," Anayake said to Wesakaychak. "As soon as the Sun is free."

"I shall call a council of all the animals upon the earth," Wesakaychak said. "*Some*one must have the courage to creep close enough to cut the cord." So he sent word across the earth, and the animals came. They gathered in the shade behind a hill and listened.

Wesakaychak told them what the Sun and North Wind had promised. Then he said, "For that brave animal who frees the Sun, I shall have fine gifts." But even before he had finished, a cry rang out from the crowd.

"I will do it! I will do it!"

An ugly little animal scuttled out between the legs of the larger beasts. The crowd laughed and snorted and howled to see him stand up on his short hind legs, and puff out his bare chest in pride. His eyes were beady, his teeth small and snaggly. The hair on his back was as sparse and bristly as a pig's. His tail was a thin little thing.

"*You*, Beaver the Braggart?" the other animals scoffed.

"No one else dares try," the odd-looking little beast shouted over the laughter. "But Beaver is brave!"

What could Wesakaychak do? No one else had stepped forward. Only Beaver. So Wesakaychak sighed and nodded. "Do your best, Friend Beaver," he said.

Beaver trotted off with his head high. Some of the animals growled as they watched him go. They said, "That little ninny will hide somewhere out of sight. He will never go near the Sun." But others shook their heads. "Sometimes," they said, "a fool can do what a wise man will not dare."

The animals held their breath and waited. Suddenly, the shadow they stood in vanished. They looked up and saw the fierce golden ball of the Sun rise above the hill. They cheered as it soared higher and higher, and moved slowly to the west. From that time to this, it has risen and set every day. As Anaynake promised, it has never since then flown too high or too low.

But where was Beaver?

He was a sad sight when they found him. Of his teeth, only three broken stubs were left. His skin was scorched. His bristles and the hairs on his tail all were burned away.

"Poor Beaver! Brave Beaver," the animals cried.

Wesakaychak stooped to place his hand on Beaver's head, and to stroke his back.

At the first stroke, Beaver's hurts were healed.

With a second stroke, Wesakaychak dressed Beaver in the finest and smoothest of fur coats. Then he gave him beautiful big, broad, flat teeth, perfect for cutting down trees for the dams he built across streams, to make ponds.

"Hoh! Beautiful Beaver!" the animals exclaimed.

They never laughed at Beaver again. Because of Wesakaychak's gifts, Beaver the Braggart became Beaver the Builder and Beaver the Busy, a hard worker, and rich. He was admired by all—and still is.

Beaver and Muskrat Change Tails

Malecite

Now, Beaver had a fine, long tail, but he admired Muskrat's short, broad one. When he was at work on his dam or playing in his pond, Beaver loved to dive. For diving, his thin tail was no help at all. How he wished to dive deeper!

Beaver's friend Muskrat cared more for speed. Muskrat longed to swim fast as a fish. But, he grumbled to himself, how could he? How could he, when he had a broad, flat tail to drag behind him?

"What a handsome tail you have," Beaver said one day.

"What a handsome tail *you* have," Muskrat replied.

Beaver's whiskers twitched. "We could trade, if you like."

"Oh, yes!" cried Muskrat.

So there and then, Muskrat put on the long, thin tail, and swam away in a flash. Beaver took the broad, flat tail. He was so pleased with it that he played half the day. He dove, and as he swam, he slapped the water with his beautiful new tail. When he went back to work, he found that it was perfect for slapping on the mud that made his dams strong and smooth. No tail in the world could be better!

Some say that soon after they traded, Muskrat asked Beaver to trade back, but that Beaver refused.

He must have, for they are still wearing each other's tails.

Wesakaychak Rides on the Moon

Cree

One night long, long ago, Wesakaychak, as the Cree call Manabush, lay on a moonlit hillside and smiled as he looked up at the beautiful sky. Its dark fields were strewn with bright stars, too many to count. He made a circle with his thumb and first finger and looked through that circle. Even in that small space, there were too many stars to count. As the round moon rose higher above the next hill, it gleamed like a great pearl. He was filled with wonder at its beauty.

"What a marvel the moon is as it rolls across the sky!" said he to himself. "If only I could ride it as it goes! I could see all of my world in one night."

"And why not," Wesakaychak thought as he sprang to his feet. So he set off at a run toward the faraway hill at the edge of the sky, where the land touched the moon's path. He ran and ran, then walked and walked. He walked all night long, and at sunrise came to the edge of a large lake. The edge of the sky was still far off. "Surely," thought Wesakaychak, "there must be a way to catch the moon!" All that next day long he paced up and down as he tried to think of one.

When evening came, Wesakaychak sat down by

the side of the lake to wait for the moon to come up. As he waited, he watched a crane land on the water. When it folded its wide wings and waddled up onto the shore, Wesakaychak saw the answer he had been looking for.

"Hold, Little Brother Crane!" he called. "Do you see over the faraway hill, where the moon is coming up? If you will carry me up to the moon before it rises too high, I will reward you well."

"Then I will," said Crane, and he flapped his wings. "Hold on to my legs, and we will be on our way."

Wesakaychak took a tight hold of the bird's strong, short legs. As Crane left the earth and soared up toward the moon, his broad wings beat strongly. On and on he flew, but it was a long while before the moon seemed closer. Crane's wings began to be weary. Wesakaychak's arms were so tired from holding tight that they trembled. Still Crane struggled on.

"Oh, hurry, Little Brother!" Wesakaychak cried. "My hands grow weak and want to let go!"

"Aw-wrk!" croaked Crane. He did not have breath enough to answer that they were nearly there. A moment later, they landed with a crash. They had no strength left to lift their heads. For a long while they lay on the edge of the moon and did not move.

Wesakaychak opened his eyes first. He found

that he was still holding tightly to Crane's legs. To his surprise, he saw that on the long flight up into the sky his weight had stretched his friend's legs as long and thin as willow wands. "Hah!" he exclaimed, with a laugh. "Now you will be able to walk much faster, Little Brother."

Crane looked at his new long legs with pleasure. "O-hoh! And I shall be able to wade in deeper water when I fish," he said.

"Very well," Wesakaychak replied. "Since they please you, all cranes shall have such legs from this day on." Then he thanked Crane for carrying such a heavy load as high as the moon. As a reward, he painted a handsome red spot between the bird's eyes. Crane looked at his reflection in the moon's shiny pearl surface, and was twice as pleased as before.

"Farewell, then!" Crane said. "I must go show my new legs and my spot to my friends." As he spoke, he spread his wings wide, then dove off the edge of the moon.

Wesakaychak peered over the edge to watch him glide back down to the earth. He was sorry to see him go but, after all, the moon did not have room for two. He stood up to look around him at its beauty.

The moon ground beneath Wesakaychak's feet was bumpy, but even the bumps were smooth and shiny. The dark sky all around was as speckled with stars as if the Creator had spilled out a great basketful. Wesakaychak saw his father, the Great Dipper, and his mother, the Little Dipper. The faraway blue-and-green earth was there, too, as small as a baby's ball. And how swiftly and smoothly his shiny round moon swept across the sky! Wesakaychak lifted his arms and shouted for happiness.

"Beautiful Moon, I shall live here on you all my life!"

For a few days, Wesakaychak was happy. But, after a while, he noticed that every day the moon grew a little thinner. Soon, he had no room to stretch out to sleep. Before long, he could only sit with his knees up. At last, the moon shrank to such a sliver that there was room only to stand. Wesakaychak had to hold tight to the moon's upper horn to keep his feet from slipping off the bottom. What was he to do? He had no wings. How could he return to the earth?

Before he could think of a way, the moon vanished from under his feet.

And he fell.

Head over heels, he spun and tumbled, and fell.

The earth came up fast beneath him, and Wesakaychak flapped his arms in fright. "Oh, Earth!" he called out. "I made you! Hear me, and make me a soft place to land! I made you new after

the Flood. I saved you. Oh, quickly, make me a soft place!"

The earth heard and hurried to obey, but there was little time. Wesakaychak fell, headfirst, into the earth's first soft spot. He spluttered and squirmed in its thick, soggy softness. He thrashed and kicked to be free of its watery tangle of plants. When at last he stood on firm ground, he dripped with water and mud. His moccasins squelched at every step.

"That is not what I meant," he shouted. "A curse on such good-for-nothing soft spots!"

But the earth liked them and made more. We call them *muskegs,* or bogs.

Woodpecker and Sugar Maple

Lenapé

Not long after the world was made new, after the animals chose their new homes, and the trees and plants grew strong and green, Sugar Maple began to itch. Dozens of little beetles had decided to make their homes under his bark. They nibbled their way in, and tunneled in all directions. When their eggs hatched into grubs, the grubs tunneled, too. The itch was so bad that Sugar Maple moaned and swayed and twisted in torment. When he tried to scratch his itch, all he could do was shake his branches and shiver his leaves. The dozens of beetles became hundreds, then hundreds more, and they all nibbled away busily.

"Help!" cried Sugar Maple when he could stand it no longer. "Someone—anyone—everyone—*help!*"

Many animals passed through the forest as they went about their daily business, but none offered to help.

"Itches are terrible," said Squirrel, "but I am too busy. My storeroom is only half full of nuts."

Porcupine shook his head. "You must be miserable," he said. "Because of my spines, I cannot scratch my back when it itches, either, but I cannot help you now. I am late home for dinner."

"You'll feel better tomorrow," Beaver called as he bustled by. "Keep busy. Try not to think of it."

Sugar Maple groaned. Perhaps, if the animals could not help, the birds would. "Help!" he called. "You feathered people—Hummingbird—Hawk—oh, *help!*"

But the birds, when they came, were no help. "What can we do?" they asked. "If you had lice, we could pick them off. If you had feathers, we could preen them. But you do not, so what can we do?"

Then Woodpecker came.

"Grubs? Under your bark?" He cocked a bright eye. "Yes, I can help. So can my cousins." So he flew away, and returned with Flicker and Downy Wood-pecker.

They pecked away busily at Sugar Maple's bark. They picked out grub after grub and beetle after beetle. *Tap-tap-ta-ta-ta-tap. Tap-tap-ta-ta-ta-ta-tap!* They pecked and pecked until Sugar Maple's itch was completely gone.

"Wonderful!" cried Sugar Maple. "I thank you all, good friends."

"We thank *you* for the beetle feast," Woodpecker and his cousins replied.

Long afterward, there came a time of drought. There was not a stream or pond or puddle to be found in the forest. The animals and birds searched far and wide for a drop of water to drink. Poor Woodpecker, half dead with thirst, came to rest on one of Sugar Maple's boughs. *"Help!"* he croaked.

"Quickly, good friend," cried Sugar Maple. "Hop to my trunk and make a hole. Make as many as you like, so that you can drink my sap when it begins to drip."

Tap-tap-tap-ta-ta-ta-tap! tapped Woodpecker. As the sweet sap dripped, he drank and drank until he was full—and found it so good that woodpeckers have been drinking it ever since.

Later, in the Second World, when men and women like us were made, Woodpecker taught them about Sugar Maple's sweet sap—and we have made it into syrup and sugar ever since.

Why Blackfeet Never Kill Mice

Blackfoot

In the Second World, the time when men and women were newly remade, the new people were weaker than the men and women of the Old World. The bird people and animal people were much greater than they. The bird and animal people were wiser, too. They had been in the world much longer. The animals lived happily, some on the plains, some in the mountains, some by lakes or rivers—but when they came together, they forgot wisdom and quarreled. Old-Man (for that is what they called Manabush) was their chief, and the birds and animals could not agree who should be chief under him. "I!" said Bear, and "I!" said Beaver. "I!" "I!" "I!" said Muskrat and Eagle and Squirrel, and others, too.

Night after night, they came together in a great circle around the council fire and quarreled. Each night the council was longer and louder. "We need a leader who can find for us all the things that we need," said one. "The greatest thief should be our chief!"

"Nonsense!" another objected. "We must choose the wisest among us as chief. Now, I—"

"The wisest?" shouted a third. "What good is

that? We need the swiftest runner, the best traveler for our chief. How else can he know how all goes with his people?"

"The greatest hunter!"

"The strongest!"

"The fiercest fighter!"

They argued on, night after night, until they were friends no longer. They screeched and shouted like enemies. Rabbit was so frightened by the ruckus that he ran off to find Old-Man.

So Old-Man came to the council and, one after the other, each animal and bird had his say. At the end, the quarreling began again, but Old-Man held up his hand and said, "Stop!"

And they stopped.

"No more of this!" Old-Man said. "We shall decide this here and now, and for good, as friends should."

With that, he opened up the sack that hung at his side, and drew out a small polished bone. He held it up between his thumb and forefinger so that it glinted in the firelight.

"This bone I hold will end your quarrel," he said. "Do you all see it?"

"We see it," they replied.

"Good. Now it is in my right hand, but you must watch it and my hands sharply. They can be as swift as Lizard and as cunning as Snake."

Then Old-Man began to sing, and as he sang he

slipped the bit of bone from one hand to the other so quickly that his hands seemed to flicker in the air. Then he stopped singing and held out both hands, tight shut.

"Hoh! In which hand do I hold the bone now?" he asked.

"The right!"

"The left!"

"No, no—the right!"

"Bear," said Old-Man, "you wish to be chief. Tell us which hand holds the bone." Bear squinted up his eyes and chose the left hand, but when Old-Man opened it out, there was no bone to be seen. Old-Man smiled as everyone laughed. Then he sang his song again, and began to pass the bone from hand to hand.

"Friend Beaver," he said, "you, too, wish to be chief. Which hand holds the bone this time?"

Beaver grinned a toothy grin and answered, "Why, your right hand. I saw you pass it."

So then Old-Man opened that hand right under Beaver's nose—and it was empty. Everyone laughed again, and Bear loudest of all.

"You see," said Old-Man. "It looks easy, but it is not. Now I shall teach you all how it is done. When you have learned it, each will play the game with all the others. When you discover which of you is the best player of all, that one shall be my underchief. Forever."

Some were clumsy and dropped the bone, and said they didn't really want to be chief anyway. Most, like Bear, played well with a little practice, but not well enough. Beaver was better than Bear, but at last Buffalo guessed which of Beaver's paws held the bone. Then Buffalo took the bone and called on Mouse, the last of all, to say which hoof held it. Now, Mouse's eyes were bright and quick, so Buffalo tried his best, but Mouse won at first try.

According to Old-Man's rules, Mouse had won, and Mouse was chief. He looked very, very small as he walked to the center of the council circle to stand beside the fire.

"My brothers—I know you think I am too small to be your chief. I think so, too. I am no warrior. I could not lead raids on enemies. I don't want to *have* enemies. I only wish to be snug in my nest with my wife and children. So I choose to give away my right to be chief. I give it to First New Man, whom Old-Man made like himself."

And that was that. Man was chief forever over all the birds and animals.

And *that* is why the Blackfeet never kill mice.

GROUND SQUIRREL
AND TURTLE

Cheyenne

Back in the time when Men were still new in the world, four of them saw Ground Squirrel and Turtle walking together at the edge of the woods. They chased after them and caught them.

"Kill them!" cried one man.

"No, let's eat them!" another said.

"I don't know," said a third. "Is that what they are for?"

"Let us ask," the fourth said, and he turned to Ground Squirrel and asked, "What are you for in this world?"

"I—um—I dance," Ground Squirrel chattered. "Yes. That is what I d-do. I am for dancing."

They lifted their weapons. "Then, dance!" they told him.

So Ground Squirrel danced, and as he danced, he sang, *"Tse, tse, tse! Tse, tse, tse, tse!"* He danced so well that they clapped, but when he had danced as far as his hole, he jumped in.

"Take care! This turtle will run away, too!" the first man warned.

"Catch him!" urged the second.

"I have him!" the third cried, and with his foot he held Turtle down against the ground.

"Roast him!" shouted the fourth. "Throw him into the fire!"

But as the third man lifted his foot and bent down, Turtle broke free and ran toward the fire as fast as he could go.

"Stop him!" cried the first.

"He must live in fire!" warned the second.

"Then," the third said, "we should throw him in the water yonder."

"Hoh, yes! He will drown there," agreed the fourth.

They laughed as they picked Turtle up. They laughed as he cried, "No, no! Not the water!" They laughed as they threw him out into the middle of the pond.

But not while he swam away.

How Summer Came
to the North

Naskapi

In the early days of men in the Second World, it was still winter all the year long in the far northern lands. All year long, the pale sun rose in the east and hung close to earth as it rolled west toward the sunset. The people were always cold, and the children coldest of all. From Muskrat and other travelers, the people and animals heard of lands far to the south, where there was summer. Farther still to the south, the travelers said, it was summer every day. There, the magical summer birds lived, and sang from sunup to sundown. When he heard this, one small boy began to cry.

He would not stop.

His father held him close to comfort him, but the boy still cried. The animals could not comfort him. His father made him toys of wood, or bone, or stone, but the boy pushed them away. His father made him a small bow and arrows. The boy took them, but still he cried.

"I want to see the summer birds!" he cried.

The little boy wept so hard and so long that the animals who were his friends called a meeting. They decided that they would try to steal the summer birds. Then the north lands could have some summer, too. Fisher, a cousin of Marten and Weasel, asked Muskrat about the people in the south.

"Where do they live?" he asked. "What houses do they live in? What do they do at night, after they eat?"

So Muskrat told all that he knew from his travels. "And after they eat, every night they dance until morning."

"What do they do with the summer birds while they dance?" asked Fisher.

"They keep them in a basket cage. When they dance, they put the basket in a bag. They hang the bag from a lodge pole," Muskrat answered. "When they are done with their dancing, they look to make sure no strangers have crept near. If they catch a stranger, they hold him and burn his nose in the fire."

So the animals who were friends of the small boy took a vote to decide whether they would keep their noses safe at home, or go south to steal the summer birds.

They decided to go.

The journey was long, but at its end they reached the camp of the people in the south who guarded the summer birds. The animals with teeth good for it went first to the shore of the lake. There they gnawed holes in the canoes of the people, and chewed on their paddles.

In the camp, in the center of the circle of lodges,

the people danced in a ring. Fisher crept close to keep watch. Owl flew up and peered down through the smoke holes of each lodge to spy out the one where the summer birds were kept. His beak was burned black, but he found the lodge at last.

At sunrise the next morning, the dancers began to tire. The animals had a plan and were ready. "Go!" said Weasel, and Muskrat set out across the lake with a big branch in his mouth. Just as they hoped, an old woman looked out and spied him as he swam.

"Come, everyone, come!" she cried. "A moose with great antlers is swimming across the lake!"

A moose meant meat for all, so the people of the south took up their bows and arrows, and ran off to kill it. They leaped into their canoes and as they took up their paddles, many of the canoes sank. Many paddles broke. In this confusion, Owl led the animals into the village. Fisher bounded into the lodge and snatched the sack of summer birds. One old woman who had not gone to the lake saw them and shouted out. "Hoh! Help! Hoh!" she cried. "Animals are stealing our birds!"

The people jumped from their canoes as they sank, and swam to the shore. They ran after Fisher and his friends, and caught up to Porcupine first. Because of his spines, they feared to capture him, but they kicked him hard on his rump. That is why he still has a humped back today. When they caught Otter, they were so angry that they trampled on his back until he was long and flat, and so he still is. Fisher ran faster, and when the people came close, he fled up a tall tree.

"I see him! Shoot him!" one cried.

"Let Whitefish shoot. His aim is best," cried another.

"I can see only his tail," Whitefish said, but he shot and hit Fisher in the tail. Fisher gave a great yelp and leaped high into the sky. As he flew up, he dropped the bag, and the basket flew open. The summer birds flew off to the north. But, poor Fisher! He had jumped too high, and he never came down. In the sky, he became the constellation the Naskapi call the Fisher.

When the other animals returned to the north, they met to decide how long they should ask the summer birds to stay. Caribou said that they should stay for one month for each of his hairs, and everyone laughed. "There are not that many *days* in a year!"

"Well, then," Caribou said, "we should have as many months as there are hairs on my tail."

"That is still too many," Porcupine said. "Let us have as many months as I have quills."

"No, no," said the others. "Too many. Too many!"

"I have it!" cried Three-Toed Woodpecker. He held up one foot and then the other. Each had three toes. "Let us have half a year of summer weather, and let that be a month for each of my toes."

So they voted and it was agreed. The north would have six summer months and six months of winter. The people of the south at first were very angry, but after a while they sighed and shrugged their shoulders. "It is not so bad," they said. "The people in the north may have spring and summer now, but in six months the birds will fly back to us."

The small boy in the north was happiest of all. His summer birds had come! He loved the warm weather they brought. When he heard that in six months they would fly south again, he was very unhappy. In secret, he took the bow his father had made for him and an arrow, and he shot a white-throated sparrow and skinned it. Then he put on the sparrow's skin, and he sang a sparrow song. When his father came to look for him, he found only the boy's clothing and the bow and arrow. Then he heard the sparrow's song, and it pierced his heart.

"My son!" he cried. "Is that you?"

"Yes, my father." The sparrow came to perch on his father's hand. "I will stay near you until the autumn. When the summer birds fly south, so shall I, but I promise that each year I will return in the spring."

The father's heart ached, but he knew how his small son had longed for the summer birds. He knew that he loved them more than anything in the world. So the father sighed. "Let it be so," he said sadly, and the man and his sparrow son went home together.

THE WHITE FAWN

Miami

Wolf went out hunting one day and killed a fine, fat doe. He ate as much as he could eat, and then sat back in the tall grass with a satisfied smile. "Ah! How fine a place the world is," he thought. He stretched out and rested his head on his paws, but just as he began to doze off, he heard a small bleat and sat up to peer through the grass. Not far away, he saw a young fawn poke its head out from the bushes where it had lain in hiding.

"Mother!" it called.

The wolf stepped out from the grass and spoke in a voice like honey. "Your mother is gone on a journey, little one. I have come to care for you until you can join her."

The fawn moved out into the sunshine, and Wolf saw that it was a little doe and that she was as white as milk. He licked his lips at the sight, but since he was not hungry, he decided to keep her until she was taller and meatier. Besides, as she frisked around him on her neat little hooves, she was as pleasant to watch as any wolf pup. Her whiteness was so dazzling in the sunshine that he wished he could have just such a coat.

The next day he took Fawn with him when he

went to visit his uncle, Fox. "Uncle," he said, "Life is good, but it would be perfect if only I had a coat the color of Fawn's."

Fox looked at Fawn. He narrowed his eyes and licked his lips. "Nothing could be more simple," said he. "All it takes is a good, hot fire. Look yonder, where the last storm's wind blew a wide track through the trees. What you must do is to set two rows of the fallen trees afire. Then, when the flames are hot and high, run as fast as you can between them. It will hurt a little, but when you come out at the far end, you will be as white as she."

Wolf did not mind a little pain, so he did as Fox directed. However, he was so eager that he could not wait until the flames reached their highest and hottest. If he had, he would have burned to a cinder, as Fox had hoped. Instead, he staggered out at the other end, coughing from the smoke, and burned almost bald. *"Oo-oo-oooo-OOOH!"* he howled.

Fox, who had been ready to gobble Fawn up, swallowed his disappointment and wisely slipped away.

Wolf staggered to the nearest stream, for a good, long drink. Little Fawn followed close behind, for she feared that her friend might vanish like her mother. Poor Wolf was too weak to move. For weeks, he lay hidden on the grassy stream bank and ate only mice. For weeks, Fawn nibbled on wild lettuce and young leaves close by, and came when he called. In time, Wolf's strength returned. His coat grew in, too—but, alas, only streaked with white. Fawn grew long-legged and nimble, but no matter how far she wandered, she always returned to Wolf's side.

"You are foolish, Friend Wolf," said his friends, Panther and Bear. "Look how she runs. You should hobble her legs or tie her fast to a tree, or one day soon your dear dinner will be off and away. Better still, we should eat her at once."

"Nonsense," said Wolf. "She is more obedient than any pup. Besides, she is a gangly thing now, all bones and pretty white hide. Never fear: Once she puts some meat on those bones, I shall have myself a feast."

That day came, at last, when the fawn was grown to a doe. Wolf sent word to all of his friends—except Fox—that they were invited to share in his feast. They met a short distance from Wolf's den, to settle on who would eat what, so as to prevent any quarrels at dinner. One was to have the tongue, one the heart, and so on down to the hooves. They did not know the white doe was close by. She heard every word. At first, she did not understand that the heart and hooves they talked of were her own. When she did, she sprang up and raced away across the plain.

Turkey Buzzard, coming late to the meeting,

saw her go. "Your dinner has run away, over the grasslands and into the woods," he told Wolf.

Wolf was not worried. "She goes that way every day. She will be back in time for dinner."

But she was not. Wolf paced up and down. His friends growled and grumbled. At last they grew tired of waiting and headed for home. Wolf set to sniffing out the white doe's trail. When he caught the scent, he set out at a run. After a while, he came to a clearing where men dressed in shirts and leggings were at work storing their seed corn in pits.

Wolf slowed to a walk. "Good friends," he said sweetly, "have you seen my daughter, a young white doe? She is late coming home, and night will fall soon."

The village chief gave a nod. "We saw her run past. If you search west through the woods, you will find her trail."

Wolf thanked him and ran on.

Once Wolf was out of sight, the men helped Doe from the pit where they had hidden her.

"Friend Doe," the chief said to her, "you must flee at once. Wolf is clever, and when he does not sniff out your trail, he will come this way again. You must run to the east. There you will come to a wide, swift river. You must be brave and swim across, then climb to the top of the tall cliff that hangs over the stream. There, you will find a trail that will lead you to the deep forest where the deer live. You will outrun Wolf easily. He is a slow swimmer and poor climber."

White Doe thanked the men, and did as their chief advised, until she reached the rim of the high cliff. When she came there, she did not run on, but stayed to watch the riverbank below. As much as she feared Wolf's fangs, she remembered his kindness, too, and wished to see him one last time.

At last, Wolf dashed out of the woods. Nose to the ground, he sniffed out the spot where she had entered the stream. When he looked in the water, he saw the reflection of the white doe on the cliff above and mistook it for Doe herself. His dear dinner was swimming away! The shimmer on the water seemed to make her shake, and he mistook the shaking for laughter.

"How dare you laugh at me, ungrateful Fawn! I have you now!"

In his rage, Wolf gave a great leap out into the water, but instead of sinking his teeth in his dinner, he struck a rock and sank. In a moment, the river snatched him up and swept him downstream through the rough rapids and away.

Fawn gave a sigh, and went on her way to the deep forest. There she met others of her own kind, and learned how to be a real deer.

And Wolf was never seen in his old country again.

THE GREAT BEAR HUNT

Fox

Long, long ago, on an early winter morning, three young men went out to hunt. The first snow had fallen the night before. At dawn it was ankle-deep, and as white and soft as goose feathers. The three brothers came out of their lodge at sunrise. They stepped through the snow single file, and after the third and youngest came the first hunter's little dog. His name was Hold Tight.

The hunters followed the river awhile, then went up through the woods a way, where they spied a trail of paw prints.

"Bear!" whispered the first young man. He smiled as he thought of the taste of the fine fat meat.

So they followed the trail up along the side of a hill, where it wound its way through a tangle of low, thick bushes. At last it led them to a cave, a hole in the hill as high as a boy of ten is tall.

"Bear's den," whispered the second young man. He smiled as he thought of the feel of a warm bearskin robe.

"Which of us will go in to drive him out?" asked the third. He frowned as he thought of the darkness inside, and the bear's sharp teeth and his long, sharp claws.

The others thought of them, too, but at last the first, who was oldest, said, "I shall."

So he went in on his hands and knees, for that was easier and more quiet than stooping. When he came to the back of the cave, he found the bear asleep, and gave him a hard jab with his bow. The bear lumbered to his feet, and the hunter gave him another hard jab. The bear turned and ran.

"Here he comes!" the first hunter shouted.

"There he goes!" called the second.

"See how fast!" cried the third and youngest.

"*A-rooo!*" howled Hold Tight, and they all ran after the bear.

"Hoh!" cried the youngest. "He is going to the north, to the land the cold comes from!" And the youngest ran even faster to the north, to turn the bear back toward his brothers.

"Hah!" called the second hunter. "See where he comes! He has turned to the east, to the land where the morning comes from." So he raced off to the east, to turn the bear back toward the others.

"Hai!" the oldest shouted. "Now he is going to the west, the land where the sun settles down to sleep. Hurry, brothers!" And he and his little dog, Hold Tight, dashed off toward the west, to turn back the bear. The others were close behind.

The brothers, all three, kept their eyes on the bear, and not on the path beneath their feet. Up and up it led, and it shone as bright as sparkling snow. At last as they ran, the oldest brother looked down and saw that they had run up the Milky Way, the Spirit Path into the sky.

"Look!" he cried. "Our Grandmother Earth lies far below us. The bear has led us into the sky! Come, brothers. We must hurry down before it is too late."

But they had come too far already. Below them, clouds floated over Grandmother Earth. All around them were heaped the hills of the Land Above, and they could no longer see the path. In their anger, the three hunters sped after the bear and shot him. "At least we will not go hungry here," they told each other as they cut up the meat. As they worked, the bear's blood dripped down onto the maple and sumac trees on Grandmother Earth, and that is why maple and sumac trees turn bright red in the autumn.

When they had finished, the hunters hurled the bear's head away into the sky in the east, where it is still. Just before first light on winter mornings, a group of stars much like the shape of a bear's head hangs low in the east. The three hunters threw his bones away, too, and at midnight in midwinter, his backbone still hangs in the north, studded with stars.

All the year long their hunt still goes on in the sky. You must look for four bright stars in the shape of a square and three bright stars and a very small, dim one following after. The square is the bear. The three are the hunters. The little one almost too small to see is Hold Tight, the little dog.

Together they still circle the sky. If the hunters cannot catch the star-bear again, they and little Hold Tight must run on and on forever.

How Glooskap Defeated the Great Bullfrog

Passamaquoddy

Long ago, a little village sat beside a brook, far from the sea and the wigwams or thoughts of other men. The people lived well there. Every day the men tied feathers in their hair, then took up their bows and arrows and went out to hunt for bear or deer. The women tended their gardens and tidied their wigwams, and carved beads out of bone and shell and stone. The children played in the sunshine.

Now, all of this good fortune came from the brook. Without it the people would have had no village at all. In all the hills for miles around, there was not another stream, or a swamp, or a spring to be found. After a rain there were rain puddles, but that was all. No one minded this, for the water of their brook was sweeter and clearer and more sparkling than any water in the world. The people were proud of it.

Then, one year, in the month of falling leaves, after a great rain, the children found that they could cross the brook by stepping from one rock to the next. "The water is lower!" they cried.

"It cannot be," the mothers said. "Such a thing has never happened."

The next day, the women who came to the bank of the brook to wash pots found the water more shallow still. "Our children are right," they said. "The water *is* lower."

And the day after that, when the men came with their nets to fish, they found the fish flopping in shallow pools. "How low the water is!" they exclaimed. They began to be afraid.

Every day the water grew lower still, until at last the stones at the bottom of the stream were as dry as bones. "Where has our water gone?" the people cried. "What can we do?" Some of the oldest people remembered stories of a lost village far up the stream, but no one had ever been there. No one knew what people lived there. "But they may know why our brook has run dry," the chief said. "We must learn from them what there is to learn." So the people chose He-Runs-Like-a-Deer as scout, and sent him up the dry stream.

High up, in a mountain valley, He-Runs-Like-a-Deer came to a great dam. Behind the dam lay a wide pond, and beside the pond stood a town of twenty poor wigwams. Sad-faced people sat in the doorways. Their gardens were yellow and brown with thirst.

"Why have you built this dam?" He-Runs-Like-a-Deer asked the people. "It steals our water, and it does you no good that I can see."

"You must ask our chief," the people said, and

they pointed across the dam. "It was he who made us build it."

So He-Runs-Like-a-Deer crossed the dam. In the shade of the great trees on the far side, he found the chief, a huge monster of a man, lying in the mud. He was a giant, ugly, and fatter than forty men together. His head was squat, with a mouth from ear to ear. His yellow eyes were as big as giant plums. His feet were wide and flat, with ugly, bony toes.

He-Runs-Like-a-Deer was afraid, but he spoke up bravely. "Chief, your dam has stolen the water of our village far below."

The monster gave a laugh like a croak.

"What do I care?" he roared. "You can drink stones. You can eat bones. What do I care?"

"But our cornstalks are brown, and our bean plants are dead. Our old people are weak, and our children weep for water."

The monster slapped his feet in the mud. His huge belly shook, and he laughed loud and long. Then he picked up an arrow, and sprang to the dam in one leap. With the arrow, he bored a small hole through the dam, and a little trickle ran down into the dry creek bed.

"There is your water," the monster roared. "Now, up and be gone, or I'll beat on your bones and bash you with stones. Begone!"

So, He-Runs-Like-a-Deer returned to his village

below, and the little trickle of water followed him. His people cheered when it came, and ran to fill all their pots. But after a few days, the water stopped once again. A few days more, and things were worse than before. The summer sun was fierce. All the people could talk of was water.

The great Glooskap—as they called Manabush—came to know of their trouble, for he had made mankind, and he could hear their thoughts. He was pleased when the people held a council and decided to send their bravest warrior to the village in the mountains. He heard the chief say, "If the people above will not help our bravest man to break the dam, then he must fight the monster and break it alone. But which of us is brave and fierce enough for that?"

Now, Glooskap always loved a good fight, and since he could go where he wished, he wished himself to the village at once. When he stepped into the council circle, the people drew back in fear, for he was ten feet tall and terrible. He wore a hundred feathers in his long scalp lock and carried a spear. His face was painted red, with rings of green around his eyes, and large clamshells hung from his ears.

"Surely," the old people cried out, "this is Mitche-hant, the evil manito, in the shape of a giant Wabanaki!"

The young men said, "Perhaps," but they thought him wonderful.

The young women said, "Perhaps," but they thought him beautiful.

"*I* am Glooskap, and I am fiercer than your fiercest warrior," Glooskap boomed. "*I* will go, and you will have your water back." And he strode off up the dry streambed, leaving the people greatly excited.

"Oh!" said one. "If Glooskap sends us all the sweet, sparkling cold water we want, what will you do? *I* want to live in the cool, clean mud and never be hot and dry again!"

"Oho! *I* want to dive in from the rocks above, and drink as I dive," said another.

"O-hoh!" said a third. "Not I. I want to swim and swim and swim, and never leave the water."

While the people were busy wishing wild wishes, Glooskap came to the village by the dam. The people hid in their houses for fear of him. Only one small boy stayed out-of-doors to stare. Glooskap sat down on a log by the fire circle.

"You, boy!" he roared. "Fetch me a cup of water, for I am as thirsty as sand in the sun."

"Oh, Master, I cannot," the boy answered. "We have none. Only our chief has water to give."

"Then run to your chief and tell him that I wish for water. Quickly, or I shall come for it myself!"

The boy ran off, and Glooskap sat on his log and waited. And waited. And waited. When at last the boy returned, he carried a small gourd cup half full of water so muddy that Glooskap threw the cup aside in anger. The people peered out their doors as the great manito rose to his feet. They watched in wonder as he strode across the dam, for he grew taller and taller as he went.

"Hoh, you!" Glooskap roared when he saw the monster sitting in the mud. "Give me a drink! Give me of the sweetest and clearest and best, you stinking sack of slime!"

"Pah! Begone," the water chief croaked. "Go drink the salt sea, if it's water you want. This water is mine."

At that, angry Glooskap grew high as a tall pine tree and lifted his spear. With a *whoosh!* he hurled it at the monster's great, fat belly—and *Hoh!* Water rushed out in a river. The monster, he saw, had made himself huge with the water that should have flowed over the dam. So Glooskap snatched the chief up and squeezed until he was small and squat and crumpled—and when he opened his hand, there was Bullfrog! And that is why to this day the bottom of Bullfrog's back is wrinkled.

Glooskap laughed to see him. "Now you will never swallow the earth's waters again!" And when he had broken the dam, he threw Bullfrog into the stream that poured down the valley.

When Glooskap returned to the village below, the stream ran strong and clear and bright, but it was full of strange new creatures. He saw scarcely a man or woman or child, for all the people who had wished for happy lives in the water had been given their wishes. They had become leeches who lived in the mud, the first in all the world, and little spotted frogs who leaped and dived, crabs who scuttled, and fish of all kinds who swam and swam and swam, some all the way to the sea.

THE LAND OF THE NORTHERN LIGHTS

Abenaki

The Grandfathers of the Abenaki learned to play ball from a boy.

Chief M'Sartto, whose name means "Morning Star," had a son, and this boy was a great worry to him. When other young boys gathered to play at games of hunting and hiding and stalking, M'Sartto's son never joined them. Instead, he took up his bow and a handful of arrows and went into the forest alone. Always he went toward the north, and always he returned after three days, or four. "Where have you been?" his parents asked, and "Why do you go?" and "What did you see?" He never gave them an answer. He never brought home rabbits or squirrels as young hunters do. Each time he came home with as many arrows as he took away.

Every time the boy went into the forest, the chief and his wife worried until he returned. At last, M'Sartto said to his wife, "We cannot let him wander into danger. Next time, I will follow him. I will bring him home." So, the next time, he took his own bow and his own arrows, and followed his son.

Chief M'Sartto followed his son north all day. The boy's path took the chief farther north than he had ever traveled before. Then, at sunset, suddenly, between one step and the next, M'Sartto's eyes closed. His eyes closed, and he could no longer hear anything. Not the rustling of leaves. Or the calls of birds. Or the sound of his own footsteps. His mind felt as empty as a new basket.

By and by, the chief's eyes opened onto a strange country. No sun shone in its sky, and no moon, or stars. There was light, but it was strange, and dim, and not at all like daylight. The people who gathered around him were not at all like his own people. They were friendly, but the words they spoke were not like the speech of his own people. Chief M'Sartto looked for his son, but did not see him. Where was the boy? What was he himself to do?

After a while he came to a field where the young men and boys of that country were playing at a wonderful game with a round ball. Never had he seen such a game. The ball and the sticks seemed to turn the air into many colors. The players all wore lights on their heads and brilliant belts braided of the colors of the rainbow. After a while, as he watched, an old man came to join him, and spoke to him in his own language. "You are new here, I think," he said. "Do you know where you are?"

"No," Chief M'Sartto answered. "I do not."

"You are in the land of Wababan, the country of the Northern Lights. I came many years ago."

"How did you get here?" asked M'Sartto, who did not know how he himself had come. "What way did you walk?"

"I came by *Ketàguswowt,* the Spirits' Path, the Milky Way," the old man answered.

M'Sartto nodded. "I must have come by that same path. Did your mind grow empty as you walked it?"

"It did," said the old man. "I could not see or hear."

Are we dead, then? M'Sartto wondered, but he feared to speak it aloud. "I came to find my son," he said, "but lost myself on the way. Can I get home again?"

The old man nodded. "Yes, the chief of Wababan will send you safely there. There is one other here from our world below, a boy, and he comes and goes."

"My son!" M'Sartto's heart jumped up in gladness. "Where is he?"

"Look for him there on the playing field, for he is playing ball," the old man told him. "Do you see him?"

"I do," M'Sartto said. "I see him! The boy wearing the brightest light is mine!"

So the old man and Chief M'Sartto watched the wonderful game. When it was finished, they went to the lodge of the chief of the Northern Lights. The old man explained to the chief that M'Sartto, a chief from the Land Below, wished to take his son and return to his home. "And so he may," said the chief of Wababan. He called his people together to bid the travelers farewell, then cried out in a great voice, "Come, my *K'che Sipps!*"

Two great birds came at his command. They took M'Sartto and his son upon their backs, and flew with them down the long Spirits' Road. As they went, M'Sartto felt his mind empty out like a jar of pouring water. When he could see and hear once again, he found himself in the forest, near his own village. When he came to his house, he found his son there before him, and his wife full of joy at their return.

The following day, M'Sartto told everyone why they saw Northern Lights shimmer in the night sky, and M'Sartto's son taught the wonderful ball game to all of the children of the village.

And he never returned to the Land Above.

The Seven Wise Men

Lenapé

Long ago—very long ago—seven wise men lived among the Lenapé. They were wise in all things of the Old Time and of this Second World, of the World Below, and of the World Above. Because of their wisdom, the people pestered them from dawn until nightfall with questions. They brought them their fears, their dreams, and their worries. The wise men were weary, and old, but they could not eat a meal alone in peace. They could not fish on the riverbank, or talk together over an evening fire. The people gave them no rest.

At last, tired of having no time to themselves, the seven wise men met in secret one night, on a hillside not far from the village. "What must we do," they asked each other, "to have ourselves to ourselves?" After much talk, one offered a plan, and the others agreed.

So they turned themselves into seven great stones.

The people missed them greatly.

Then, early one evening, a clever and curious young man from the village came walking across the hillside. He saw the seven oddly shaped rocks

and was puzzled. He did not remember seeing them on the hill before. "Hoh!" he said. "I do not remember you." And he touched the first rock as he leaned close for a better look.

"Haa!" The rock woke up. "Who touched me?"

"O-hoh! A stone that talks?" The quick-witted young man counted the other rocks. "Five, six—seven!" he crowed. "Surely I have found our seven lost wise men."

The seven great stones groaned. "Oh, not so loud, young man! The people will hear you."

So the young man sat himself down at the center of the circle of rocks, and in low voices he and the seven wise men talked for a long while of many things—of why deer have short tails, why the Northern Lights dance and shimmer, and of many other questions great and small. When the shadows grew deep, and it was time for the young man to be gone, he promised the wise men that he would tell no one that he had found them. "For," they said, "it is many years since we have had such pleasant, restful days as these, drowsing on this hillside."

The young man kept his word and held his tongue, but the wise men's peace did not last for long. After a few days, the people began to wonder where the young man went each evening. They saw that he went always in the same direction. "I will follow him and see," said one man, and he did. He could not creep close enough to hear what was said, but he returned to the village and told how the young man sat talking to seven large stones.

"He has found the seven great wise men!" the people cried. "Tomorrow let us rise at dawn and go to the hillside to hear their wisdom."

The seven wise men sighed when they saw them coming.

The next evening they held council once again among themselves. If they were to have peace and contentment, they decided, they must leave the village and its valley behind. They must find a new home. So they journeyed far into the forest. There, they turned themselves into seven beautiful cedar trees. For a long while, the only visitors they had were the birds who perched on their boughs. In time, though, some hunters passed by. They saw the seven cedars. They had never seen trees so tall or so beautiful in that part of the forest, and they returned to the village with the news. "Surely we have found our seven wise men," they said.

The next morning, the villagers went to see the seven trees, and knew that the hunters were right. So they sat beneath the cedar branches, and begged the wise men to share their wisdom.

That night, the wise men were hoarse from talking. They held council among themselves, and decided that they must find a new country, where the villagers could not follow. But where?

While the seven old men stood in the forest and pondered, the Creator looked down on them and took pity. Sweeping them up, He carried them into the sky, where He turned them into seven bright stars. And they are still there, where we cannot pelt them with questions or disturb their peace.

You call them the Pleiades.

THE BURNT-FACED GIRL

Micmac

Teäm the Invisible and his sister lived near a large village beside a lake. Now, Teäm's sister was an excellent cook, and she kept their wigwam clean and comfortable. Even so, Teäm wished to be married. He was invisible, but his feelings were the same as any young man's. Because he wished for a wife, his sister wished it, too. But how was he to court a wife when he was invisible night and day?

"I cannot," said Teäm. "But somewhere in the world there is a young woman who can see me. Find her, and I will marry her."

So the sister of Teäm the Invisible let it be known in the village that any girl who could see her brother might marry him.

At this, there was great excitement. Almost every girl who did not have a husband was curious enough to try. Every evening that winter, at the hour when the men returned from hunting, Teäm's sister walked home from the village. Every evening, one or two girls joined her.

"Here comes my brother now," she would say as they walked along the lake. "Do you see him?"

Now, some spoke truthfully, and said, "No." Most answered, "Yes." To those who said, "Yes,"

Sister would say, "Tell me, then, of what is the cord that pulls his sled made?"

"Of a long strip of rawhide," said some, for that is what most sled ropes were made of.

"Of braided thongs," said others.

Teäm's sister did not say so, but she knew that these were guesses, or lies. She said only, "Come, help me prepare his supper, and eat with me."

In the lodge, she warned the girls which seat was Teäm's. When he came, he did not speak, but they could see that he was a real person. When he took off his moccasins at the door, they became visible. When the meal was cooked and served, Teäm's food moved through the air and vanished. They watched in wonder, but no matter how long they stayed, they never saw even an eyelash of the young man himself.

Now, at the other end of the village, there lived an old man with three daughters. His wife was long dead. The two oldest daughters were tall and handsome, but the youngest was small and weak, and often unwell. Her sisters did not care for her as a mother would have, and as sisters ought. Instead, the older sister teased and punished her, and burned her with hot coals. The second sister was not so cruel, but she was not kind.

The poor child was scarred all over her arms and legs and face from her hurts. The villagers called her Oochigeaskw', the Burnt-Faced Girl.

When the father came home from hunting, he asked each time why the smallest was injured. Each time, the oldest said that she had warned her sister to stay away from the fire. "But she would not. She stumbled and fell in, poor child."

The two older girls were now young women, and thought themselves very fine. When they heard that Teäm the Invisible wished for a wife, they danced for joy. "Surely one of us will be able to see him," they said. "Surely we are meant to marry great men." So they combed out their long hair and put on their finest embroidered skirts and jackets and leggings. They pulled on their rabbit-skin stockings and sealskin moccasins. They put on their cloaks with beaver-skin sleeves. Then they went out to find the sister of the Invisible One.

Sister was on her way home by the path along the shore of the lake. The two girls ran after her, and walked with her until Teäm passed by. "There he is," said Sister. "Do you see him?"

"Of course," said the first girl.

"I, too," said the second.

"That is good," said Teäm's sister. "Tell me, of what is his sled cord made?"

"Of rawhide," both said together, but their lies did them no good. They stayed to help cook his dinner, but they never saw even one hair of his head.

All the next day, they were angry. When their

father came home, he came with a gift, a pouch full of the shells from which wampum was made. The two older girls divided the shells between them. "We will make pretty beads to brighten our belts," they said. They left none for their sister.

While they were busy at their work, Oochigeaskw', the poor little burnt-faced girl, brought out an old stiff pair of her father's moccasin boots. She put them to soak in a pot of warm water, to make them soft enough to wear. Then she crept up beside Second Sister and whispered, "May I have some shells, too?"

"Go away, ugly creature," First Sister snapped. But Second Sister gave Oochigeaskw' two shells. Then, because her skirt and jacket were only ragged skins, the smallest sister slipped away to the forest. There, she cut for herself sheets of birch bark. From the bark she made leggings and a side-stitched dress with a shell on each shoulder. She put on these new garments, and then her father's moccasin boots. The boots came almost to her knees. Her half-burnt hair stood up in spikes. Her thin little face was burnt and scarred. Yet she set out bravely through the village, to try to see Teäm.

The people laughed and hissed and hooted as she passed by. Her sisters came running to see what the noise meant. When they saw her, they shrieked out that she shamed them. But Oochigeaskw' went on, for her heart was strong.

At Teäm's house, Sister came out to meet her. "Let us walk by the lake," she said, and they walked until Teäm came toward them. "Do you see him?" Sister asked.

"Oh, I do," the Burnt-Faced Girl whispered. "And he is as beautiful as the sunrise."

"And his sled string—what is it made of?"

"It is—it is the Rainbow." And Oochigeaskw' began to be afraid.

"Yes, my sister," the other said, "but tell me of his bowstring."

Oochigeaskw' trembled. "His bowstring sparkles like the Milky Way, the Spirit Road."

"You have seen him!" cried Sister. She hurried the Burnt-Faced Girl home with her, and there she bathed her. As she did so, the burns and scars on the girl's face and body washed away. Sister combed her hair, and as she combed, the girl's hair grew long and gleamed like a blackbird's wing. She stood straight and tall, and her eyes shone like stars.

Then Teäm's sister placed her in the wife's seat, next to the door. When Teäm the Great stepped through the door, he saw her there, and smiled as he sat down beside her.

"Welcome, Wife," he said.

THE BEAR MAIDEN

Ojibway

Long ago, deep in the woods, there lived an old man and an old woman. They had three daughters. The two older daughters were beautiful, and the youngest was a little bear.

In time, the old man grew too old to hunt, and the old woman too old to work with the girls in their cornfield. When autumn came, they did not have enough food for the winter to feed all five.

"We must leave our home to find work or find husbands," said the oldest sister.

"Yes," said the next. "If we do not, how will we care for our parents?"

"I will come, too," piped up the little bear.

"No," her sisters said quickly. She was a good little animal, but they feared that people would not welcome them if they came with a bear at their heels.

"There is corn enough for our father and mother in the baskets, and dried meat enough hangs from the lodge poles," said the little bear. "I will come, too."

"No," said her sisters. And they left her at home.

They had not gone far when they heard a *pad, pad, pad-pad* behind them. They turned to see Little

Bear hurrying after them. "No," they said. "You may not come." So they took her home and tied her to one of the doorposts of the wigwam, then left again to look for work.

In no time at all, they heard a *bump, pad, pad, bump-bump!* behind them. When they turned, they saw their sister dashing after them with the doorpost bobbing on her back. "No, Little Bear," they said. "You cannot come." So they took her home again. There, they tied her to a strong pine tree near the wigwam, and once more set out on their journey. They had not gone a mile from home, when they heard a *crash! crash! swish-crash!* When they turned, they saw Little Bear running after them with the pine tree bobbing on her back. More than ever, they did not wish her to come with them. They were sure that she would shame them. So they tied her to a great rock beside the path, and went on their way.

Before long, they came to a river too wide and too fast to cross. "What shall we do?" they asked each other. Neither sister had an answer, so they sat down on the bank to think. Then, as they sat there, they heard a *thud! thud! thud-thud!* behind them. At the sound, they turned to see their little sister trotting toward them with the great rock teetering on her back.

The two older sisters thought for a while longer, then they looked at each other and sighed. They rose and went to untie the rock. Then, between them, they lifted it up and threw it into the middle of the stream. Together, they pushed a fallen pine tree out across it. Then they looked at each other and sighed again.

"Come, Little Sister," they said. And they stepped out onto the pine-tree bridge, with Little Bear following after.

At sunset, the three sisters came to a wigwam in a dark part of the forest. An old woman sat in the doorway. As they came near, she asked where they had come from, and where they were going.

"Our parents are old," the oldest girl said. "We must find work, so that we may care for them."

"My two daughters have cooked supper," the old woman said. "Come, eat, and stay the night."

Little Bear growled, for the old woman smelled like a witch, but her sisters did not listen to her warning. They went in to eat, for they had walked all day and were hungry. They ate, but Little Bear took not a sip of supper, for she saw a finger bone in the soup. At nightfall, Little Bear stayed up when her sisters and the old woman's daughters went to bed. She stayed up and watched the old woman, and told her stories until the old woman fell asleep. She snored, but Little Bear gave her a small pinch to make sure that she slept. Then she went to the bed where the four big girls were sleeping, her sisters on the outsides, and the old woman's daughters between them in the middle. She lifted them up, and

put her sisters in the middle, and the old woman's daughters on the outsides. Then she lay down by the fire as if she were asleep.

In the middle of the night, the old woman arose in the dark. First, she pinched Little Bear to make sure that she was asleep, and Little Bear gave a small snore. Then the old woman drew a knife from her sleeve and crept to the big bed. Little Bear listened. When the witch returned to her own bed, Little Bear waited until she fell fast asleep. Then she rose, and awakened her sisters, and together they crept away.

The next morning, the old witch-woman awoke and found that she had killed her own daughters, and not the little bear's sisters. She was so angry that she leaped up to the sky and pulled down the sun. She ran with it to her wigwam and hid it so that the two sisters and Little Bear would lose their way in the dark. But the three sisters went on by moonlight. By and by, they met a man who carried a torch.

"I am looking for the sun," the man said, and he told them that his village was nearby. When the girls and the little bear came to the village, they saw many people with torches. The people were unhappy, for their chief had fallen sick when the sun disappeared. When they told the chief that the two girls had a little bear for a sister, he called her to him.

"Bear, can you bring back the sun?" the chief asked.

"Yes," said Little Bear. "But you must give me two paws-full of maple sugar now, and your oldest son after." So she took the maple sugar back through the woods to the witch's wigwam. There, she climbed up to the smoke hole. From the smoke hole, she dropped the sugar into the pot of wild rice that cooked on the fire below. When the old woman came to taste the rice, it was too sweet. She poured out the sugar water and went out to fetch more, fresh from the spring. At once, Little Bear slipped into the wigwam. She took up the pot in which the sun was hidden, and ran out to throw it up into the sky, higher than it was before.

When Little Bear returned to the village, the chief was well again. He gave her his oldest son, as he had promised, and Little Bear gave the young man to her oldest sister, to be her husband. But all was not well. When the old witch-woman saw that the sun was back in the sky, she was angrier than ever. In a rage, she jumped up into the sky and ripped down the moon. Soon, the good old chief fell sick again, because the nights were so dark.

"Little Bear," he asked, "can you bring back the moon?"

"Yes," she said. "But you must give me two paws-full of salt, and your second son."

When she had the salt, the little bear ran off to the witch's wigwam and did the same thing as before. When the witch went out for more water,

Little Bear slipped in, snatched up the basket in which the moon was hidden, and tossed the moon high in the sky. On her return to the village, the grateful chief gave her his second son, as he had promised, and Little Bear gave the second young man to her second sister, for her husband.

But not all was well. The next day, the old chief's favorite horse disappeared, and the old chief fell sick from grief.

"Little Bear," he said, "can you bring back my beautiful horse with the silver bells in its mane and its tail?"

"I can," said the little bear, "but you must give me two more paws-full of maple sugar, and your youngest son." When she had the sugar, Little Bear went off to the witch's wigwam and did as before. When she slipped into the wigwam, she found the horse and set to untying his bells. In her haste, she missed one, and as she led the horse out through the door, the little bell tinkled *tling! tling!* The old woman heard it, and ran back to catch Little Bear. "Hoh-hoh!" She laughed as she put Little Bear into a deerskin bag, and tied the bag to the branch of a tree. "Hoh-hoh!" she laughed as she went off to the woods to find a club to beat on the bear in the sack.

But Little Bear had sharp claws. She tore a hole in the bag and jumped down. She untied the last bell on the horse. Then she popped the witch's dogs and her pots into the bag and tied it up. As she led the horse away, she heard the yelps and the cracking of pots as the witch-woman beat the bag.

Back in the village, Little Bear took the beautiful horse to the chief. He gave her both his youngest son and a wigwam close to her sisters and their husbands. But Little Bear's own husband had no wish for a bear for a wife. He scowled, and spoke not a word. She growled in anger, but he would not eat what she cooked. When night fell, he turned his back on her, and lay down to sleep on the far side of the fire. At that, poor Little Bear reared up on her hind legs and roared: "If you do not wish a bear for a wife, then throw me in the fire!"

So he did.

Little Bear's sisters heard the noise and came running.

"What has happened?" they cried. "Where is our sister?"

"She told me to throw her into the fire," the young man said. "And I did."

After Little Bear's sisters went weeping away, the young man heard a sudden sound behind him. He turned, and saw a young woman as beautiful as the moon and stars step from the flames. "Oh, Little Bear!" he cried in joy.

But Little Bear turned her back on him, and lay down to sleep on the far side of the fire.

KUPAHWEESE'S LUCK

Lenapé

Once, many years ago, in a Lenapé village beside a wide river, there lived a man named Kupahweese. He was a lazy, boastful, foolish man. He was poor, but he never gave a thought for tomorrow. Most of the time he was too lazy to hunt, and tried to borrow food from his neighbors instead. Now, his neighbors had long ago learned that he never repaid the turkey or trout or roast of venison they gave him, and so they always said, "No!" His promises were worth nothing. In spite of all this, Kupahweese was good company. He loved to play ball, to laugh, and to sing, so his neighbors liked him even though he was a lazy do-nothing. His guardian spirit was patient with him, too, and generous.

One day, Kupahweese took too much to drink, and began to boast to his neighbors. "You think you are rich, but so am I. *I* am so rich that I will give a feast for all of the village!"

"You, Kupahweese?" The young men laughed. "And what shall we eat at this feast? Roast pine log and grass soup?"

Kupahweese was offended, but just then he saw his only cow—his only cow and his wife's dear pet—pass by on her way home to be milked. "There!" he cried. "There is our feast. Kill it, and skin and clean it, and I will build the fire for the roasting. Only put the tripe to one side, for me to take home. I do like tripe!"

So they killed the cow, and when they cut out the tripe to clean it, what did they find inside but a fancy coat sewn all over with silver buttons. "Hoh, Kupahweese!" they cried. "See what your cow has swallowed."

Kupahweese was delighted. He cut off the silver buttons and gave them to his wife to sew on her blouse and skirt, so that she would not weep too long for the cow. With all her bright buttons, she was the best-dressed woman at the feast.

Sadly, it was not long before the buttons were gone. Kupahweese, with his lazy, careless ways, traded them, one by one, for this little thing or that, until he and his wife were as poor as ever. One morning he lay late in bed, and moaned that he was ill. "Oh, Wife," he groaned, "what I need is a bowl of good, strong soup."

"I have nothing to make it with," answered his wife. "We have not a bite of bird, nor a bone of bear or deer, and nothing to trade for a morsel or two."

"Hoh!" sighed Kupahweese. "If I were not so weak, I would go catch a fish."

Now his wife had no time to catch him a fish, for she had all the garden to dig. So she brought him his rod and line, and caught him some grasshoppers for bait, and helped him down to the riverbank. For a long time he sat, and dozed, and dreamed of soup. Then, suddenly, he thought he felt a tug on his line, and his eyes flew open. He gave his pole a great jerk, so that his line flew high over his head, to the top of the hill. After a while, he gave it a tug. To his surprise, something tugged back.

"O-hoh!" thought Kupahweese. "It must be a great fish indeed, to be so strong out of water!" So he followed the line to the top of the hill. There he found not a fish, but a fat turkey gobbler that had swallowed the grasshopper and hook as they flew over the hill.

"Ho-*hoh!*" Kupahweese exclaimed, for he liked turkey soup much better than fish soup. So he killed the turkey, and began to clean it. Just then, he heard a loud *honk-honk!* and looked up to see a flock of geese fly low overhead, and swoop down to light on the river. They sat on the water just where he had been fishing.

Kupahweese licked his lips. Goose was even fatter and tastier than turkey. If only he had his bow and arrows! He stretched out in the grass and watched the geese, and wondered how best to get one. "I am a good diver and swimmer," he thought at last, "and I can hold my breath a long time—"

So he took up his fishing line and went a little way upstream. There the geese could not see him slip into the river. He swam fishlike through the water until he slid under the geese, and saw their feet paddling over his head. Gently, he tied a loop around one goose's leg. It was so easy that he tied another, then two more, then three, and still more until at last he had to come up for air. He popped up with a great *whoosh!* and a splash and a gasp.

The geese were so frightened that they all took off at once, and Kupahweese snatched at the fish line to haul them down again. Instead, the tangle of line looped around his wrists, and the geese flew off with Kupahweese sailing behind.

"Help!" he wailed. "Great Spirit, help me! Must I die for being greedy? Surely it is not so bad a thing as that?"

The geese flew on. They flew upriver toward a place where a steep cliff loomed up at the water's edge. Now, a tree grew atop that cliff, and a raccoon was dozing on one limb of that tree. Half of the geese flew over the branch, and half under it. They got in such a tangle that the raccoon was tied fast and strangled. Kupahweese clung to the branch with one hand while he pulled the other free of the fish line. Then he switched hands and freed the other—but as he did so, he lost his hold and fell, feet first, into the river.

But Kupahweese's luck was with him. His long fall was broken by something just under the water. When he caught his breath, he looked and saw that it was a great fish. A monster of a fish. It was the largest fish Kupahweese had ever seen, and his fall had stunned it. So he waded out of the water to find a pole to help him roll it safely ashore, where he could come back for it later. Then he climbed the cliff to kill the geese and untie the raccoon to take them home. On the way, he stopped to collect the turkey.

"Husband!" Kupahweese's wife exclaimed when she saw him weighted down with game. "I thought you went fishing!"

"So I did," said he, "but the turkey took the bait, and I had no bow to shoot the geese, so I tied their feet together, and they killed the raccoon, so I fell in the river and stunned a great fish, then rolled him onto the land, and here I am."

"So you are," said she, and she went with him to butcher the fish and carry the meat home. But when they cut it open, they saw that the monster fish had swallowed a bear that must have been trying to cross the river.

"It's a good, fat bear," said Kupahweese. "Bear meat is better than fish."

"And we will have fat for cooking and oil for our skin," said his wife.

So they took the bear home and left the fish for the birds. When the meat was dried, they had enough to last until spring, and Kupahweese could be as lazy and thoughtless as ever.

His neighbors shook their heads at his story, and smiled and sighed.

"That Kupahweese!" they said. "Such a liar!"

THE MIGHTY WASIS

Penobscot

There came a time, at last, when the great
Glooskap had rid the world of all the wicked beings
who roamed it. He had killed the last of the giant
Kewahqu', who were wicked wizards. He had killed
or chased away all of the wizards the people called
m'téoulin. After that, he had set out to battle the evil
night spirit, Pamola. He won that fight, too. Sometimes he went out hunting for his enemies.
Sometimes they came looking for him. In every fight
it was Glooskap who won, for his magic was greater.
At last, the day came when he had beaten all of the
witches, ghosts, man-eaters, and monsters in the
land. At last, men and women were safe from all
such dreadful demons. Glooskap was almost sorry.
He had worked hard, and now that he was finished,
he did not know what to do next.

"I would like—something to eat," said he to
himself.

At the next village, the great chief of men and
beasts stopped at the first wigwam he came to. The
woman whose house it was gave him soup and meat
to eat, and she listened with wide eyes to his tales of
the spirits and creatures he had tricked or defeated.

"But now my work is done," Glooskap said with

a sigh. His sigh shook the house. "There is no crea-
ture good or bad, in this world or in the World
Beneath, who dares to defy me. No one can conquer
Glooskap!"

When she heard this, the woman laughed. "Do
not say so, Great Glooskap! I can name one not
even you can outwit or overcome—one who will
have his own way from now until the world's end."

Glooskap frowned. "Impossible. Who is this
dreadful giant?"

"He is the Mighty Wasis." The woman hid her
smile with her hands. "He sits behind you here and
now. Take care! Meddle with him if you dare, but
only if you hunger and thirst for trouble."

Glooskap turned with a scowl.

The Mighty Wasis sat on a mat by the wigwam
wall, and sucked on a lump of maple sugar. He gig-
gled and gurgled to himself as he sucked, for he was
the woman's baby.

Now, Glooskap, the Maker of Men and Women,
had no wife and no child. Because he was always
busy with Great Things, he never bothered to look
at a child when he saw one. Still, he was Glooskap
the Great. His powers were stronger than any man's,
large or small. Silly goose of a woman! He could
handle six such little ones with his hands tied. And
with a basket over his head! So he held out his
hands and smiled a smile sweeter than maple sugar
and honey together.

"Come, little man. Come to me," he said.

The baby smiled, but stayed where he was.

Glooskap made his voice warble and trill like a summer bird's. Then he cheeped and chirped like its chick. Then he chucked and chattered, *Come, come!* in the speech of the squirrel people.

Wasis sat and sucked at his maple sugar.

"Very well," Glooskap said. He drew himself up to a great height, and growled like a bear. "Crawl over here, Worm," he roared, "or I shall gobble you up in one gulp!"

Wasis screwed up his eyes and screamed and bellowed until his face turned red, but he did not move.

Since nothing else worked, Glooskap gave up and tried magic. He chanted his strongest spells. He sang the songs he used to frighten evil spirits and the ones to wake up the dead. Wasis only sat on his mat and listened. He listened as if he had never before heard anything so interesting, but he did not move.

"I give up!" Glooskap groaned in despair.

Little Wasis clapped his hands and crowed, *"Goo, goo!"*

Forever after, and even now, when a baby laughs at nothing and crows, *"Goo, goo!"* it is because he or she remembers that long-ago time when a baby defeated the great manito who watched over all the world.

GLOOSKAP'S FAREWELL GIFTS

Micmac/Passamaquoddy

Even though Glooskap's work was done, he was not pleased with it. The mighty monsters and giants were gone. The great, dark-winged Cullo and the horrible Chenoo of the North no longer terrified men and women and children and animals, or ate them. Wicked beasts and snakes did not lurk outside their doors. More than that, Glooskap had taught people how to hunt and farm and fish. He had taught them arts and skills that made them happy and comfortable, too, but were they thankful? They prayed to him, and spoke as if they loved him, but all that was words. In their homes and villages, many of them lied, or were lazy and thoughtless, or were so spoiled that each wished the world would go *his* own way.

At last, Glooskap grew so tired of the selfish ways of men and animals that he called for his messengers, the Loons. When they came, he told them, "Fly out across the world, and tell all the peoples— men and animals, fish and birds—that one day I shall leave this earth. Say, too, that to anyone who can find me, I will grant one wish, no matter what that wish may be."

So the Loons flew away north and south and

east and west, carrying the news to every wigwam and house, every cave and nest, every lake and river, roost and burrow.

After they heard of the Great Glooskap's offer, many creatures, mostly men, set out to find him. The way was long and wild, the weather terrible, and the dangers deep. Many failed, but among those who tried were a Malecite man and two Penobscots. Others turned back after a year or two, but not they. Each of these three jogged on, and on, through hunger and hardship, through deep drifts of snow and thick summer clouds of mosquitoes. After seven years, one day they heard Glooskap's dogs barking from afar, and their hearts rose. Every day the barking grew louder as they drew nearer. The way was still hard but, after three months more, they came at last to Glooskap's camp.

Glooskap was pleased that they valued his gifts enough to dare the journey. He made them welcome, and prepared a fine meal. Afterward, and far into the night, he told them tales of his adventures. Not until the next morning, as they prepared for the journey home, did Glooskap ask what their wishes were.

The first to speak was the oldest. "I am a simple man," he said, "and poor. My neighbors shrug their shoulders and say that it is because I am a poor hunter. Therefore I ask, Master, that you make me a great hunter and killer of game."

"I will," said Glooskap, and he gave him a magic flute carved of dark wood. "Every animal will come to you when you play this flute."

"I thank you, Master," said the first man, and he set off for home.

"And you?" Glooskap asked the second man.

"I," the second man answered, "wish to have the love of many women."

Glooskap frowned. "How many?" he asked.

"Hoh!" said the man, who had never been able to win a wife. "I don't care how many. Enough. No, more than enough!"

Glooskap shook his head, but smiled as he brought out a small bag tightly tied with a cord. "Take care! If you open it before you reach your own village, you will wish you had never made such a wish."

"I understand," the man said eagerly. "Thank you, Master." And he turned and hurried toward home.

The third man was a merry, good-looking young fellow, cheerful and more silly than wise. To Glooskap's question, he answered, "I wish to make people laugh. People love to laugh. I can do funny laughs and funny sneezes, but if I could make the Marvelous Noise to go with my songs, they would love me and ask me to every feast and merrymaking."

Now, the Marvelous Noise is impossible to

describe except by making it. Unless there is still some old magician deep in the woods who knows it, and throws it out among the trees to please the bears and owls, it has gone from this world forever. It was not a comical noise, but a sound both odd and wonderful, weird and joyful. Everyone who heard it, even the sourest and saddest, burst into laughter. They felt their hearts lift and their burdens lighten, and they laughed.

"Very well," said Glooskap. "You shall have it."

Glooskap whispered a command in the ear of his friend Marten, and the marten scurried into the woods to seek the magical root Glooskap had named. When he returned, Glooskap took the root from him, put it in a leather pouch, and tied the pouch up tightly.

"This root," he explained, "gives the knowledge of the Marvelous Noise to those who eat it. But, I warn you! Do not touch the root before you reach home. If you touch it with so much as the tip of your littlest finger, you will be sorry indeed."

"I understand," the young man said eagerly, and he set off for home at a run.

Now, it had taken seven years for the three seekers to find Glooskap but, though they did not know it, home was only a seven days' journey away. The merry young man sang as he ran, and was so happy to be on his way home that he entirely forgot

Glooskap's gift until he stopped to rest. Then the pouch that hung from his belt reminded him. He opened it up without a thought for Glooskap's warning. Without a thought for what might happen, he took out the root and ate it.

At once, he knew that now he could make the Marvelous Noise, so he opened his mouth and made it. The sound rang through the forest and over the hills, and all the birds and beasts answered with something like laughter.

"Hoh-hoh-hoh!" cried the young man in delight. "How all the people will love me!" And he leaped up and bounded away toward home, as merry as a flock of grackles. All the while, he sent the Marvelous Noise on ahead of him as far as his voice would carry.

After a time, though, the young man began to be bored. He wished for something new to be doing. Before long, he spied a deer not far off. He put an arrow to his bow, and crept quietly nearer, to shoot it. But just then, as he raised the bow and sighted along his arrow, *oh!* the Marvelous Noise leaped out of his mouth.

The sound rollicked and rolled among the rocks and through the trees like a wicked witch's warble. The deer gave a leap and a bound, and was gone.

"*Lahmkekqu!*" the young man cursed, and he went on his way.

By the time he reached the first village on the

way to his own, he was weak with hunger. He had barely enough strength to greet them with a Marvelous Noise, but they laughed with joy on hearing it, and he felt a bit better. They took him in, and fed him, and laughed. At first. But the young man's Marvelous Noise kept bursting out. Again and again and again. In the middle of a meal, so that they could not eat. In the middle of the night, so that they could not sleep. The poor young man himself could not eat, or hunt, or sleep, and soon the people had laughed themselves weak and wished him gone. So he went on his way home, but lost his way and starved to death before he came there.

The second man, who could not win himself a wife, had no better luck. He was so happy to have Glooskap's gift that, as soon as he was safely out of sight in the forest, he took the pouch from his belt and opened it. At once, hundreds of girls flew out in a great swarm, girls with long black hair and fierce black eyes. They fought to fling their arms around him. They struggled to kiss him. "Hoh, don't stop! Don't stop," he cried.

But soon they became wilder, and crowded closer, until he was buried under a great heap of girls. "Stop, stop," he gasped, but they would not. He struggled to escape, but he could not move.

The next travelers who came that way found him dead. But there was no sign of a single girl.

Of the three men who set out on their way

home, only the first finished his journey. The hunter who could not shoot straight kept his magic pipe in his pocket, for he remembered Glooskap's warning. He sang to himself as he trotted along, for he trusted Glooskap's word. He knew that for the rest of his life he would be a fine hunter, and his family would never go hungry. That was worth waiting for.

Glooskap was surprised by the hunter's good sense, and pleased. "Hoh!" said he to himself as he left the earth and climbed into the sky. "Perhaps making men and women was not a mistake after all."

ABOUT THE STORYTELLERS

THE ALGONQUINS

The tales retold in *Turtle Island* come from only a portion of the numerous tribes that make up the Algonquian peoples. (*Algonquin* is the noun form of their name, and *Algonquian,* the adjective. One of the tribes is known by the same name, but to avoid confusion, their name is spelled *Algonkin.*) Many tribes—like the Chowanoc, Conoy, Mahican (often now called Mohican), and Powhatan—vanished, with their stories, in the century or so after the arrival of the Europeans. In some cases, survivors took refuge with neighboring tribes and in time lost their own traditions and tales. As time passed and the Algonquian peoples dwindled or were scattered, still more were lost. Not until toward the end of the nineteenth century did Native American and white scholars begin to record the tales, some of which I have retold in *Turtle Island.* The storytellers are from the following tribes:

ABENAKI
Their name is really Wabanaki, "those living at the sunrise." When the Europeans arrived, most of the Wabanaki lived in western Maine and part of

New Hampshire. Because of their connection with their neighbors—the Penobscot, Pennacook, Malecite, and Micmac peoples—these too are sometimes called Abenaki. Their traditions tell that they came into what we now call New England from the southwest. In the French and Indian Wars, they sided with the French against the English, and after their defeat moved north into Canada, where the French still ruled.

BLACKFOOT

The Blackfoot nation—the westernmost of the peoples who spoke Algonquian languages and the largest of the tribes of the high northern plains— included three tribes, or bands: the Blackfeet (or Siksika), the Bloods, and the Piegan. The name Blackfoot supposedly came from their custom of painting or dying their moccasins black.

According to Blackfoot tradition, their ancestors came from the north to what are now Montana and the province of Alberta in Canada. Unlike the other plains dwellers, they were nomadic hunters even before the late seventeenth century, when the Indian trade in and use of horses began to draw other Plains Indians away from farming and villages into the nomadic life. The Blackfeet followed the buffalo herds and raided American settlers, but did not as a tribe make war against the U.S. Army. In the nineteenth century, however, the great slaughter of buffalo by American and Canadian hunters was as disastrous for the Blackfeet as war. In Canada, many also died in epidemics of the "white disease"—smallpox. Today, Blackfeet still live in Montana and Alberta, but on reservations that are only remnants of their old homelands.

CHEYENNE

Cheyenne is the Dakota Indian term for "red talkers," meaning "people of strange speech," but the Cheyenne thought of themselves as "the Beautiful People." According to their traditions, before 1700 the Cheyenne lived on the Minnesota River, then moved up into North Dakota. There, and later along the Missouri River, they lived in villages, growing corn and making pottery, but as they moved south and west toward the Black Hills, they grew away from the settled life and became nomadic hunters. In the mid-1800s they split into the Northern and Southern Cheyenne. Both took part in a number of the desperate Wars for the West. Most were killed in massacres or in battles, and the survivors were sent to reservations in Montana and Oklahoma.

CREE

When the French first met the Cree, in the early 1600s, their country in Canada stretched west from James Bay, at the south end of Hudson Bay, to the Saskatchewan River. The French employed the Cree as guides and hunters in the fur trade, as did the English after the establishment of the Hudson's Bay Company in 1667. Later, with their allies, the Assiniboin, the Cree pushed south into the present United States to make war against their enemies, the Sioux. They also raided to the west and north, and were followed by the fur traders. Later, because they continued to be important to the fur trade, they had better luck than most Native American peoples and were able to remain in their old territories.

Fox

The Fox people called themselves Meshkwa-kihug, the "red-earth people," for their tales told that the first Fox man and woman had been made from red earth. Their closest relations were the Sauk and the Kickapoo. The French first met the Fox people in Wisconsin, and for many years the Fox were at war with the Chippewa (Ojibway) and later with the French, allies of the Chippewa. Driven southward, they and their allies, the Sauk, in turn drove the Illinois tribes from a part of northern Illinois. In the end they settled in Iowa and some in Kansas, in the Indian Territory, with the Sauk. (The Indian Territory at first included almost all of what is now the state of Oklahoma and most of Kansas and Nebraska. It was supposed to be safe from settlement forever, but those promises were broken. Between 1854 and 1907, piece by piece, Congress opened the Indian Territory up to settlement.)

LENAPÉ

The Lenapé (pronounced *Lay-na-pay*) were called Delawares by the English. *Lenapé,* their own name for themselves, means "the true men" or "the original men." They were called Mohomis— "Grandfather"—by the Algonquian peoples, whose traditions told of their own descent from the early Lenapé. The closest of these "grandchildren" were the Powhatan, Conoy, and Nanticoke, and the Mahican, Wappinger, and southern New England peoples, but the Algonquian language family included dozens of other closely or distantly related peoples. Lenapé tradition told of the migration of their distant ancestors from far to the northwest.

When the Europeans first arrived, the three peoples of the Lenapé lived from western Long Island and Manhattan and the nearby mainland down through New Jersey and parts of eastern Pennsylvania into northern Delaware: the Munsee in the mainland north, the Unami from Long

Island and Manhattan south, and the Unilachtigo in southeastern Pennsylvania, southern New Jersey, and northern Delaware. The first European voyagers met them in 1609. The English came in 1664, and in 1682 their chiefs met in council and signed a treaty with William Penn, whom the king of England had named "Proprietor" of the Pennsylvania colony. Penn respected Lenapé property rights and was a good friend to them, but those who came after were not. The traditional enemies of the Lenapé, the Iroquois, tricked them into giving up for many years the "right" to make war. Later, the English colonists and, after the Revolution, American settlers pushed them west across Pennsylvania into Ohio, then Indiana, and in the end to Oklahoma, where most now live.

MALECITE

Their name is probably from *Malisit,* which is what the Micmac called them. It means "broken talkers." The Malecite were often grouped with the Passamaquoddy, Penobscot, Abenaki, and Pennacook under the general term Abenaki. Most lived in the Saint John River valley of New Brunswick, Canada, and some others in northeast Maine. Their tradition told that they had come from somewhere to the southwest. A hundred years after the English took Canada from the French in the mid-1700s, the Malecite were left with only small scraps of their old lands.

MENOMINI

Their name is Menomini, or Menominee—"wild rice men"—because they depended on the wild rice that grew in the lakes of their country in Wisconsin. That country was a large area centered on the river that still is known as the Menominee. Their traditions told that they came there from northern Michigan, and they held their Wisconsin lands until 1854, when they ceded most of them to the federal government in exchange for its protection. Many still live on the remnant of those lands.

MIAMI

Of the peoples of the Illinois Confederacy—the Miami, Kahoki, Kaskaskia, Mascouten, Michigami, Peoria, Piankishaw, and Wea—the Miami were the best known. Miami means "people of the peninsula"—the peninsula between Green Bay and Lake Michigan, which was their home before they moved south into Illinois. In 1763, in protest against the invasion of white settlers, they joined Pontiac's Rebellion and took British Fort Miami (Fort Wayne, Indiana). The rebellion died down, and a royal proclamation that year forbade white settlement west of the Appalachian Mountains, but it had little effect. After the American Revolution, even more settlers came. In 1790 the Miami Chief Little Turtle led the Miamis and their allies to a victory over troops sent by President Washington to stop Indian raids on settlers. Little Turtle led his warriors to an even greater victory over General St. Clair, commander of the next force sent against them, but later defeats led in 1795 to the loss of Ohio and much of Indiana to the Americans. Forced farther west in the decades that followed, they and other peoples of the old Northwest came in the end to the Oklahoma Indian Territory.

MICMAC

In their own language, *Migmac* means "allies." They were most closely related to the Malecite, Passamaquoddy, Penobscot, and Abenaki, but their language was more like that of the Cree. Their home was in Nova Scotia, on Cape Breton Island and Prince Edward Island, along the New Brunswick coast of the Bay of Fundy and—later— in Newfoundland. Norsemen may have met the Micmac on their voyages a thousand years ago. From the time of John Cabot's voyage from England in 1497, the Micmac had contact with Europeans. French missionaries came to teach them Christianity, and the Micmac became faithful allies of the French. After the English conquest of

Canada, they lost land but stayed at peace and in their old homelands.

MONTAUK

The Montauk lived in the central and eastern parts of Long Island and were to some degree dominated by the Pequot on the mainland. After the Pequot were destroyed, they were harassed by the Narraganset until they took shelter with the colonists. Epidemics and the departure of others to New York left few on the island, but some of their descendants still live there.

NASKAPI

The more northerly of the Montagnais-Naskapi people, kindred to the Cree, the Naskapi were less well-known to the French and English in Canada than the Montagnais until the nineteenth century. Like the Montagnais and Cree, they were important to the fur trade, and so were never driven from their old lands. These included the interior of Labrador and lands at James Bay.

OJIBWAY

The pronunciation (and spelling) of their name varies—it is *Chippewa* in the United States and *Ojibway* in Canada, but it is the same word. The name means "to roast until puckered up," which refers to the puckered seam in their moccasins. The Chippewa/Ojibway were a very large and widespread nation. Their traditions told of their coming from somewhere farther east, but they settled from northern Michigan and Wisconsin westward as far as North Dakota and along the Canadian shores of Lake Huron and Lake Superior. In the 1800s, like other Indian nations, they were moved into reservations, though only a few moved out of their old country.

PASSAMAQUODDY

Passamaquoddy means "pollock-plenty-place" (pollock are a kind of fish), and the people lived on Passamaquoddy Bay and along the border between Maine and Canada. After the American Revolution, most of them stayed in Maine.

PEQUOT

Pequot means "destroyers." They were a warlike people who lived along the Connecticut coast east of the Niantic River, and they ruled over and were much feared by their neighbors. After the Pequot War with the English colonists, the survivors who did not move from the region were placed under the rule of their neighbors or sent by the English to Bermuda, as slaves. The use of the name "Pequot" was banned, and the use of their names for places was forbidden.

SHAWNEE

The name *Shawnee* means "southerners," and they were relatives of the Sauk, Fox, and Kickapoo, who lived farther north and west. By the time the Europeans came, the Shawnee had moved down the Cumberland River into Kentucky and Tennessee. From time to time, they divided into separate bands. Some moved on to Alabama and Georgia, others to Pennsylvania, and then many to Ohio. For many years they were at war with the settlers. Pushed steadily westward, they came at last to Oklahoma, where most now live.

WAMPANOAG

The name *Wampanoag*, like *Abenaki*, means "eastern people." They lived mostly in the parts of Rhode Island and Massachusetts east of Narragansett Bay and also on the island of Martha's Vineyard. When the Pilgrims settled at Plymouth in 1620, the Wampanoag and their great chief Massasoit made them welcome and entered into a treaty of friendship. As more and more colonists settled on Wampanoag lands, Massasoit's son, known as King Philip, made war on the English. The Wampanoag and their allies were defeated, and more died in epidemics of the "new" diseases that came to America with the settlers. Many of the present-day descendants of the Wampanoag still live on Martha's Vineyard.

*   *   *

There are other tales still to be retold—from the Algonkin, the Kickapoo, Montagnais, Nanticoke, Potawatomi, Sauk, and others, but those wait for other winter evenings, other campfires. To learn more about the Lenapé, look for Paul A. W. Wallace's *Indians in Pennsylvania* (1981). Your public library may have it, or other books about the Algonquins or individual tribes.

ABOUT THE STORIES

Folktales and other traditional tales come down to us from the distant (and occasionally the recent) past. Some may have their roots in stories thousands of years old, and the many retellings have both polished them smooth and changed them. Even in old storytelling cultures that wished to pass their tales on unchanged, change crept in. Even when the words stay much the same, each teller tells a story in some way differently. Some "do all the voices" or use gestures or movement to add life to a tale. A story may take on a new brightness or a new grimness as one storyteller adds a comic touch because his audience loves to laugh, or another darkens a wood with shadows to deepen her listeners' suspense. Tales can die, too, as tribes or villages or old people do, or they can be rescued. The grandson who tells the tale he heard from his grandmother, and who has forgotten this part and that and patches it up from imagination or another tale, is still keeping it alive. And among his hearers may be the child who grows up to tell the tale to a person with a notebook or tape recorder who will put it into a book with other tales. And that is where I find them.

A number of the tales I have retold in *Turtle Island* come from a single version told by a member of a single tribe. Others I found in more than one version, often from storytellers from different tribes or villages or different times; for each of those tales, I chose to retell the version I felt to be either the most complete or the most interesting. In retelling some stories, I have borrowed an interesting detail or two from a version I did not choose. When I found no complete version of a good tale, I pieced together portions of it from several sources to make one. Like almost all storytellers who are "*re*-telling" the tales of other folds to audiences of strangers, rather than telling those that come from their own tribes or families, I use my own words, so that the story becomes—in a way—mine, too.

The sources I drew from were sometimes modern retellings themselves, but more often were versions recorded by travelers, early or late, or by scholars of folklore, Algonquian historians and storytellers themselves, or makers of story collections. These are some of the more helpful books:

Richard Calmit Adams's *Legends of the Delaware Indians and Picture Writing* (1905) includes "Kupahweese's Luck." Mr. Adams was himself a Lenapé.

John Bierhorst's *Mythology of the Lenapé* (1995) is one of several sources I drew on for "The Creator Makes the World," as is Chief Hitakonanu'laxk's *The Grandfathers Speak* (see below).

Daniel Brinton, in *The Lenapé and Their Legends* (1885), recounts some of the tale of "Turtle Island," but a number of details in my retelling come from other sources, including the *Wallam Olum*. The *Wallam Olum*, the "Red Record" of Lenapé history, was supposedly copied from old Lenapé pictographic records and the recital of a dying Lenapé "history man," transcribed by the traveler Rafinesque. Many scholars now believe Rafinesque's version to be a hoax, but it is based upon a core of genuine Lenapé tradition.

Hìtakonanu'laxk's *The Grandfathers Speak: Native American Folk Tales of the Lenapé People* (1994) is written by a Lenapé chief, and my own retelling of "Woodpecker and Sugar Maple" has its source in this version. Hìtakonanu'laxk has also researched and retold several other tales, such as "Rainbow Crow," which I found in a number of versions.

An article in the *Journal of American Folk-Lore* was one of the sources for "The Coming of Manabush" and "Manabush and the Monsters," in vol. 4 (1891). Articles in later volumes recorded a number of the other tales: "The Land of the Northern Lights," vol. 3 (1890); "The Bear Maiden," vol. 15 (1902); "Why Deer Have Short Tails," vol. 22 (1909); "Beaver and Muskrat Change Tails," vol. 30 (1917); "Wesakaychak Rides on the Moon" and

"Wesakaychak Snares the Sun," vol. 42 (1929); and "The White Fawn," in vol. 52 (1939).

Charles Godfrey Leland's *Algonquin Legends* (1968), originally published in 1884, includes versions of stories told to him by New England Algonquins. They include "How Glooskap Defeated the Great Bullfrog," "The Burnt-Faced Girl," "The Mighty Wasis," and "Glooskap's Farewell Gifts."

Wayne Leman, ed., in *Cheyenne Texts: An Introduction to Cheyenne Literature* (1980), includes a text of "Ground Squirrel and Turtle" both in the Cheyenne language and in a literal translation into English upon which I based my retelling.

Frank B. Linderman's *Indian Why Stories* (1915) includes the retelling of "Why Blackfeet Never Kill Mice" upon which I based my own.

Alice Marriott and Carol K. Rachlin, eds., in *American Indian Mythology* (1968), reprint "The Great Bear Hunt," "The Race between the Buffalo and Man," and many other tales in the forms in which they were recorded from Native American storytellers by earlier scholars and writers.

Robert E. Nichols Jr.'s *Birds of Algonquin Legend* (1995) includes a version of "Rainbow Crow" that was one of the sources of my own retelling.

William Duncan Strong, in *Labrador Winter: the Ethnographic Journals of William Duncan Strong* (1994), records the version of the Naskapi tale "How Summer Came to the North" that I drew on for my retelling.

Gladys Tantaquidgeon (a Mohegan scholar), in *A Study of Delaware Indian Medicine Practice and Folk Beliefs* (1942), recounts one of the many versions of "The Seven Wise Men." Another source that contributed to my retelling appears in *The Grandfathers Speak* (above).

Milton A. Travers, in *The Wampanoag Indian Tribute Tribes of Martha's Vineyard* (1960), tells the legend of "Maushop the Giant." My version is pieced together from his and a number of other brief accounts.

Mentor Williams, ed., in *Schoolcraft's Indian Legends* (1956), tells "The Three Cranberries," one of the many stories that Schoolcraft recorded and first published in 1839.

*   *   *

The tales retold in *Turtle Island* are old, perhaps

ancient, but readers may notice in several small details—a cow, a horse, silver buttons, silver bells—that some storyteller in the chain has added things in the years after the European traders, trappers, and settlers came. In one of these stories, however, ther are—perhaps—signs of something more.

In the seventeenth and eighteenth centuries, French trappers and traders, unlike the English, often married into and lived among the tribes they traded with. It is not hard to imagine those Frenchmen sitting at a winter campfire and trading tales of witches, fairies, and magic with their Cree or Ojibway friends. It is possible that "The Bear Maiden" may have come down through the years from just such an evening of campfire tales. A. E. Jenks, the gentleman who published it in 1902, heard it in the late 1890s from Pa-skin', an Ojibway woman who was over one hundred years old. Pa-skin' lived on the Lac Courte Oreille (French for "Lake Short Ears") reservation in Wisconsin, and the story she recounted was probably told among the Ojibway many years before she was born. As in many European fairy tales, its actions take place in groups of three, and most of its characters are grouped in threes. One very important adventure—the hero's saving her sisters by switching them with the witch's daughters—is a motif that appears in several old European fairy tales.

But whether "The Bear Maiden" has a faint French flavor or not, here it is an Ojibway tale, for it was and is the way of storytellers to take a tale that speaks to their hearts, and make it their own.

ABOUT THE AUTHOR

Jane Louise Curry has been writing and telling stories since the fourth grade in East Liverpool, Ohio. After high school in Johnstown, Pennsylvania, she trained at Penn State and Indiana University of Pennsylvania as an art teacher, but later went on to study English literature at UCLA and medieval English literature at Stanford University. During the summers she worked as a counselor and then an administrator at Camp Osito in California's San Bernardino Mountains, where she first learned and retold at evening campfires old tales of the California Indians. During a Fulbright fellowship year at the University of London, she volunteered to work with local children, and her storytelling led to an invitation to tell one of the California tales at an International Gathering of Boy Scouts and Girl Guides. It was the children's suggestion that she make a collection of tales to be published as a book, and that collection, her first book for children, was published in 1965 as *Down from the Lonely Mountain*. *Back in the Beforetime*, a second collection of California Native American tales, appeared in 1987. Writing about the Lenapé tribe in *Dark Shade* (1998), a novel for young people, led to her wider interest in the other Algonquian tribes and their stories, and to *Turtle Island* (1999).